I0592674

Christmas with the Boss

Annie Seaton

Dedication

This book is dedicated to my whole family.
Christmas is for family time!

Acknowledgments

A special thank you to my wonderful editor
and dear friend, Susanne Bellamy.

Chapter One

Christmas Eve

Jilly Henderson joined the end of the queue at the only gas station in the quiet little beachside town of Sandy Heads. She folded her arms and settled in for a long wait; it was Christmas Eve and it appeared everyone was stocking up on their last-minute snacks before the shops shut for Christmas Day. Glancing down, she smiled as a pair of large, tanned, sandy, *and* bare feet in front caught her attention. She straightened and lifted her eyes a fraction, enjoying the sight of tightly-muscled calves above those bare feet. Tilting her chin higher, her leisurely perusal continued up tanned skin lightly brushed with blond hair, up to firm thighs that disappeared into a pair of board shorts molding one of the most perfect male butts she had ever seen. Down south, her feminine bits that had been dormant for *way* too long gave a little jiggle.

"Always check out the size of their feet, girls. Big feet, big—"

"Sharyn!" The giggles that had gone around the office contrasted with the corporate black suits and classy chignons of the executive assistants on the tenth floor of the bank building in George Street. Between the bouts of frantic activity that happened on the trading floor twenty-four hours a day, Jilly spent most of her work day shaking her head at Shaz's antics and hilarious advice.

Blonde-haired and elegant Shaz always managed to come up with a dry comment to break the tense atmosphere of the trading floor. The one about checking out the size of a guy's feet before accepting a date had the girls howling with laughter.

'Because you know what that means, ladies!'

When the boss had lifted his head and frowned through the glass wall of his office, they all quickly put their heads down and focused on the colored numbers on their screens.

Now Jilly stared down at the feet of the guy in

front of her. Not that he'd be interested in her, but this guy had *big* feet.

Huge feet. Sharyn would say that was a yes. Jilly stifled a grin and let out a soft sigh; the pretty young things chattering away in front of him were keeping his attention on the front of the queue. Surfer boy wouldn't be interested in a tired and frazzled city girl.

She hadn't been on a date for over a year, so she hadn't had a chance to put Sharyn's test into practice. *And* those girly quivers below were few and far between these days, so that little tremble low in her belly did put a smile on her face. Memories were nice.

Jilly needed no one; she was here at the beach to have a total break. Work had been hectic leading up to the festive season, and with many nights of Christmas functions, drinks and farewells she was feeling burned out.

Five days of bliss, alone, no work and no one to bother her beckoned.

Mr. Big Feet took a step forward as the queue moved and Jilly shuffled along closer to the counter. Her gaze lingered on that tight butt, clad in snug-fitting boardshorts, before she lifted her eyes to feast on a golden tanned back. No harm in looking.

Oh, my. She swallowed.

Broad shoulders lightly dappled with freckles had a sprinkling of sand stuck to the smooth skin. Small grains were embedded in the sexy hollow at the top of his shoulder. It made her think of lazy afternoons lying on the sand. Jilly literally had to curl her fingers to stop herself from reaching up and brushing the sand away. Maybe the surf god wouldn't be impressed if a tired and stressed-looking woman with dark circles beneath her eyes ran her fingers over that glorious back. To distract herself, she turned away and looked out at the cars in the fuel bay, trying to pick which one was his.

Of course. A beat up 1970s Kombi van with two surfboards secured to the roof racks was at the front of the line. Jilly nodded to herself; that would be surfer boy's car. How good would it be to jump in with him and head up the coast to Byron Bay? That was sure to be his destination—a mecca for surf gods.

A girl could dream.

Another step forward in the queue and she turned her gaze back to him, unable to resist one last look.

His curly brown hair was sun-bleached on top, and the thick, springy curls just brushed his shoulders. Even his neck was strong and tanned.

She fanned herself as her wicked imagination kicked into overdrive and tilted her face up toward the frigid air blowing from the vents in the high ceiling. Even though artificial, the air was blessedly cool. A welcome relief after the strong smell of petrol that had pervaded the hot bay as she'd filled her car. It was just on dark, but Jilly was sure the mercury was still registering over thirty degrees outside.

Summer down under. *Bliss.*

Not to mention her internal temperature was sizzling as the erotic fantasy filled her mind. What a sad life she must lead to be fantasizing in a gas station! This short holiday was *way* overdue.

It had been a long, long drive from Sydney. The sooner she found the beach cottage and fell into bed the better. Exhaling with a tired sigh, Jilly shuffled forward another step as the queue moved at a snail pace.

"No, the party's at the surf club *tonight*."

Jilly tilted her head to the side, looking past the surf god's broad shoulders towards the girl who was chatting to the cashier. Mary, the cashier—Jilly could just see her name tag—reached for the milk that the customer had placed on the counter. The register beeped as she scanned the plastic container.

"Tonight? I thought the party at the surf club was on New Year's Eve?" The pretty young girl in a red sarong pushed her hair back from her face as she lifted the rest of her groceries onto the counter. Her voice rose shrilly.

Mary chewed gum as she shook her head—no rush here. The dozen or so customers in the queue ahead of Jilly almost let out a collective sigh as they jiggled their feet, tapped hands on thighs and looked at their watches. Even the surf god's shoulders tensed a little, sending another pleasant little ripple through her belly.

Country service.

But Jilly liked it; people-watching was fun, even if she was tired. In Sydney, you were lucky to get a hello in any store. Now Mary, the slow-moving cashier, leaned on one elbow and imparted the correct information about this party to anyone who was interested. "No, it's tonight. Starts in a couple of hours."

"Really?" The girl in the red sarong leaned forward. "Are you sure?"

"Yes, it's at the surf club *tonight*. The New Year's Eve *party* is at the pub on the river."

"Well, I'm not missing either of them. Have you seen the talent in town this week?" Jilly resisted a nod as the 'talent' in front of her stretched to his toes and the muscles in his calves flexed.

"All the local surfers are home for Christmas and the parties will be hot!" The young girl pushed her hair back from her face as she turned apologetically to the person in the queue behind her. "Sorry, I remembered I just have to grab some party supplies. Won't take a minute." She flicked a glance back to the cashier and her mouth split into a grin. "Just as well

I've already been to the bottle shop."

"Got your priorities right there, love." Mary, the cashier's, voice held a tinge of sarcasm.

"Oh, for God's sake." Impatience filled Jilly as she watched the girl head for the fridges lining the back wall. The next customer in line stepped up to the other register but Mary waved him away.

"Sorry, love. The other cashier is on a tea break. You'll have to wait." She flicked open a magazine on the counter and began to read, ignoring the cross mutterings of the waiting customers.

Jilly closed her mouth as another yawn threatened.

What was one more delay? Her day had been fraught with them since she'd hit that first red traffic light in Manly this morning. Anyone would think she was having a bad luck day. Black cats, ladders, broken mirrors, shoes on tables—her dad had been a sucker for superstitions and Jilly knew them all. She swallowed as she pushed that thought away; her grief was on hold until she was ready to deal with it.

The entire trip up the coast from Sydney had

11

been a nightmare from start to finish. Heavy traffic had choked the M1 as what had seemed like the entire population of the city, headed for the beaches of the north for the annual break between Christmas Eve and the New Year. Dad had always told her not to leave Sydney on Christmas Eve, but Jilly had been so keen to get away from the city after the funeral, she'd decided to put up with the traffic.

But it had turned into a ten-hour trip, instead of the five it should have taken. Despite the six-lane freeway, a broken-down truck near the Gosford interchange had added two hours to her trip. Finally, after crawling through slow bumper-to-bumper traffic, she'd called into a small town just south of her destination to stock up on groceries for her eight-day break. Once she got to the beach cottage, she had no intention of getting back in her car until she left after the New Year.

Keen to travel the last short leg of the trip, she'd hurried out to her small sedan with her few grocery bags and groaned. An old, battered utility had her car parked in. Jilly had sat on the grass verge in the hot sun, fuming for half an hour until an elderly couple pushed their laden trolley across the car park. The words that she'd had ready to blast the car's owner died away as she watched the old man hold his wife's hand and place her carefully in the front seat, before he slowly unpacked the trolley into the back of the ute. Jilly couldn't help herself. She pushed to her feet and helped him unload.

"Thank you, my dear." He went around to the front of the car and came back with a small parcel and pressed it into her hands. "Merry Christmas. One of Ethel's plum puddings for you."

Tears welled into Jilly's eyes and she ran the back of her hand over her face; emotion had clogged her throat for the whole trip, but she wasn't going to give in. "Merry Christmas to you and your wife too."

He drove away sedately; still oblivious that he had blocked in Jilly's car. With a sigh, she'd pulled out and hit the highway again.

Smothering a yawn with the back of her hand, she rocked on her feet as she waited and looked over to the brightly-colored products on the shelves along

13

the wall. Everything to tempt the sweet tooth she tried her best not to indulge.

Bad move. On the back seat of her car were three bags filled with salad makings, and fruit. Shaz and Elise, the perpetual dieters at work had taught her good habits; there was no Christmas cheer for her apart from Ethel's plum pudding. Jilly smiled as she stepped away from the queue. She was at the rear, so if she was quick, she wouldn't lose her place.

Picking up a basket she headed to the fridge and opened the door. A minute later her basket was filled with a carton of custard to go with the plum pudding, five small bottles of full-cream strawberry-flavored milk—she wouldn't tell the girls at work—two family size chocolate bars and two trashy magazines. Jilly stepped between the shelves and threw in two bags of potato chips for good measure on her way back to the queue. No one had joined it and she got to stand behind the surf god again.

The girl in the sarong was still loading her basket. It was Christmas; Jilly had to dig deep to find some Christmas spirit. Finally, the girl came back to the counter, paid for her party goodies and the queue began to move more quickly. There were now only seven customers ahead of Jilly and she covered another yawn with one hand.

A second cashier appeared behind the counter and the queue moved again. Jilly reached down to pick up her basket as surfer boy reached the head of the queue and paid for his fuel. Bending down, she reached for her basket as he turned to pass her. She glanced his way as she straightened. Did the face match the perfect body?

Oh. My. God.

Jilly froze and forced her open mouth to close. If you *could* freeze when prickles of heat scorched your skin.

"Miss Henderson." Her boss, the senior group executive and chair of the Executive Committee of the SBA bank stopped walking and flashed a smile at her. Perfect white teeth, the same sexy grin that she'd admired every day for the past six months. She'd tried to ignore her good-looking boss since he'd arrived at the bank mid-year. But now, the tailored business suit had been replaced with a bare chest and those low slung boardshorts, and the fantasy of the last ten minutes now left her gasping for composure. Her mouth dried as she stared at the V of dark blond hair that disappeared into the shorts below his navel. The muscles on his chest were as ripped as the rest of him. Who could ever have known what that business suit hid?

"Mr. Smythe-Phillips," she finally managed to croak out.

"Feeling peckish, are you, Miss Henderson?"

"What?" Jilly lifted her eyes from his bare stomach to meet a pair of eyes crinkled with laughter.

Sprung perving at his chest. How embarrassing.

His grin widened as he pointed to her plastic basket.

Relief flooded through her; he was talking about the food. Jilly swallowed and forced the huskiness from her voice. "Ah yes, um . . . er . . . um . . . some holiday supplies," she stuttered and stumbled over her words like a teenage girl with a crush.

Thank God, he hadn't noticed her when she'd

been salivating over him in the queue. There was no way she could have sustained a conversation with him for any length of time with him half-naked in front of her; she would have died of embarrassment. It was bad enough to be caught out in a pair of skimpy shorts, and a tight-fitting T-shirt. At least he was on his way out and she didn't have to make social conversation for long.

"See you back at the office next week. Have a good Christmas . . .Jilly." His voice was as deep and sexy as ever and her name rolled off his tongue. She'd never noticed what a sexy voice he had before.

Jilly nodded mutely.

He really was just too gorgeous; for six months she'd managed to hide how she'd dreamed about Dominic Smythe-Phillips. And that was when he was in a business suit. Now he'd morphed into a tanned surfing god, she was a goner. How the hell she'd ever sit across the board table without thinking of that bare chest when she went back to work . . .

Jilly stared after Dominic as he opened the door of the silver Audi TT Roadster that was parked behind the Kombi van. Wrong again.

Little warm tingles were having a fun time down in the now ex-dormant zone.

"Stop perving and hurry up, love. You're holding up the queue." Mary's drawl was amused as her gaze followed Jilly's. "Bit of a looker, is our Dom, isn't he?"

Jilly closed her mouth and turned to the waiting cashier.

Our Dom?

Chapter Two

Dominic Henderson turned his sleek sports sedan onto the dirt road that skirted the beach. He deliberately looked away from the first cottage and turned his attention towards the beach. Purple shadows cast by the setting sun hovered on the glassy water. The last rays caught the slow-moving swell as it pushed to shore, breaking as a bridal veil of foam on the wet sand. Even though the waves were small, there was a nice right-hand break on the point, just catching the last glimmers of light from the sun as it sank below the Great Dividing Range to the west of Sandy Heads, the small town where he'd learned to surf.

Should be great for a surf in the morning.

But surfing tomorrow wasn't at the forefront of his thoughts. The skimpy shorts and the figure-hugging tank top were very different to the attire of Miss Henderson of the corporate suits and high heels.

19

If it hadn't been for the glorious copper-toned hair that cascaded down her back, Dominic probably wouldn't even have recognized the woman behind him as his executive assistant. The lush image imprinted on his mind since Jilly Henderson had gaped up at him in the gas station wouldn't go away. The same woman who had caught his eye the day he had been appointed as chief of the Group Executive at the biggest bank in Sydney. There'd been muttered comments about special treatment when she'd been promoted to his executive assistant, but it hadn't taken much to dispel the gossip. He was used to it; corporate banking was a bitchy and cutthroat environment. He recognized talent and hard work; good looks were a bonus.

He wondered idly where she was heading and then focused on the surf. They hadn't shared their Christmas plans; the office was too busy for personal conversations. And he much preferred to keep work businesslike without the social chitchat that went on in the lunchroom.

Kept the rumours at bay. Although he did

wonder what Jilly Henderson had been up to lately. Usually one to stay late at her desk, in the last month she'd been leaving as soon as trading ceased for the day, and then she'd had a few days off last week. Personal time, she'd said with no further explanation. She got her work done, so it was none of his business.

Dominic shrugged as he turned to the ocean. And she did her work very well; she had a keen eye for the stock market and on more than one occasion Jilly Henderson had directed his attention to recent trends before he'd noticed them.

Forget work. He was here for a break.

If the swell stayed small, he'd get his knee board out and wax it ready for the morning. Didn't matter that it would be Christmas Day; he had no family left in town.

Nice legs, though.

It had probably been stupid to come up here in his rare time off from work, but it was as good a time as any to try to put his memories to rest. Long overdue.

And cute freckles too.

21

He'd hit the sack as soon as he'd waxed his board. Pleasant tiredness tugged at Dominic's muscles; he'd been in the water all day on his large board. He'd hit the surf early again tomorrow; his knee board should still be in the small wooden shed attached to the old building at the back of the cottage.

The familiar and long-loved smell of salt and seaweed met Dominic as he climbed out of the Audi. He grabbed the carton of beer he'd picked up from the pub and walked through the long grass to the old cottage. He'd have to pull out Pa's old mower while he was staying here. He stood on the front steps and looked back down the road. It had been a long time since he and Derro had walked together down that road on their way to high school . . . and to the surf. When they'd been teenagers without a worry in the world.

And it had been almost as long since he'd last been down to the other cottage: his grandparents' cottage. Not since Derro's funeral. Dominic pushed open the door and the fresh smell of the ocean was replaced by the musty smell of an old house that had been locked up for a long time.

Pretty eyes too.

He grinned again as green cat-like eyes fixed on his stomach flashed into his head. The prim Miss Henderson had been checking him out. He'd never noticed those cute freckles on her nose either. Maybe he'd break his own rule and ask Jilly Henderson out for dinner when they got back to the city.

Chapter Three

Jilly threw her junk food purchases onto the back seat next to the healthy groceries. Shaking her head, she peered up the road, but the silver Audi was out of sight.

Who would ever a thunk it? Shaz would say with a giggle. Fancy Mr. Iceberg being up here on the north coast. Shaz had soon branded the new boss with his nickname, when it became quite clear he was not up for socializing . . . or flirting. It was only last week that the girls had been speculating about where the sexy Dominic would spend Christmas. Jilly had been quiet, and her colleagues had been sympathetic about her losing Dad.

London, Paris, or skiing at Aspen had all been mooted for the boss. Slumming it north of Sydney hadn't rated a mention. What had the cashier meant by "our Dom"? Anyway, it would be fun to recount her experience of checking him out in the gas station to the girls in the office; they'd get a laugh out of that. She hadn't contributed much to the usual hilarity in the lunch room these past few months.

Then again, maybe she wouldn't tell them just how delectable he looked in his boardshorts. She'd file that little picture away for the meetings where Mr. Iceberg sat business-like in his dark suits, barely cracking a smile as he concentrated on profit margins and stock movements. Anyway, that was work; this week was for much needed relaxation and regaining her emotional strength after nursing Dad in his final days. It was time to forget about him. Jilly grinned—it was hard to compare the new Dominic with the one she was familiar with.

She turned on the GPS as she drove back onto the main road and headed for the beach. Several wrong turns and a good hour later, she finally turned onto the sandy road that led to the address on the receipt shoved into her bag. The GPS had kept telling her to turn right—into the ocean.

The sun had set, and darkness was falling quickly. She hoped the key to the rental was where it was supposed to be; the guy on the phone had been vague and hard to understand with his soft muffled voice. She frowned as a long, deserted road loomed ahead of her. Tall trees encroached on both sides and there was no sign of any houses. She stopped and pulled the receipt out: yep, that was it—Swimming Creek Road. Jilly knew she was finally on the right road; she'd seen the sign when she had ignored the robotic voice of the navigation system, followed her instincts, and turned off the esplanade.

She frowned; no luxury cottage fitting the description of Beachside Vista was anywhere to be seen. She'd checked out the holiday rental online when she'd received an email advertising a vacancy over the holiday break; the photographs had displayed the interior of a spacious cottage decorated in a retro style across from the beach. Not that she really needed spacious for the few days she'd be here. Her car moved slowly along the narrow road and the beachside she-oaks formed a dark canopy above her, and she stared ahead trying to see in the murky light.

The sandy road narrowed even more, and the

frequent potholes got deeper. Jilly shivered as a feeling of gloom pervaded the early evening. Suddenly a house appeared ahead of her to the left and she almost overshot the driveway. She hit the brakes and the car pulled to a stop. An old wooden sign hung crookedly from a post in the long grass at the side of the narrow road proclaiming she had arrived at Beachside Vista.

"Oh, no." A groan escaped her lips.

An old weatherboard cottage loomed out of the darkness as she stepped from the car. She squinted in the dim light. The paint was peeling, and loose guttering hung in a jagged, rusty spiral, scraping noisily against the side of the house. The wind had picked up and another shiver ran down her back as it keened eerily through the trees, the breaking ocean providing a mournful background.

All it needed was a storm to make it totally spooky.

Crack! Jilly jumped a foot. A clap of booming thunder instantly followed the flash of lightning that lit the sky almost as though she had summoned it.

Okay, she'd wanted privacy but maybe not quite *this* much isolation. The knee-length grass brushed against her bare legs and she turned back to the car for the small torch she kept in the glove box. Small creatures rustled in the long grass and she stepped quickly back to the side of the road. Flicking the torch on, she shone the light along the side of the old building. Sure enough, there was a small box at the side of the porch where she'd been told to find the key. Lifting the lid, she pulled out an envelope and flashed the torch on the spidery writing.

'*Henderson. Five nights.*' She shook the envelope and a large key slipped into her hand. Thank goodness, it was the right Beachside Vista, but it was *nothing* like she'd expected. It was definitely not the house in the ad.

No matter; it was close to the beach and that's where she'd be spending most of her time. Jilly shrugged and climbed the stairs. The door opened slowly with an ominous creak.

Talk about a cinematic setting. What was it going to be like inside?

Two minutes later—because that's all it took to investigate every nook and cranny of the *not*-spacious cottage—Jilly returned to the car for her backpack and food supplies. She quickly stowed her groceries in the ancient, rusted fridge on the back porch, along with the chocolate and the two bottles of wine she'd brought from her fridge at home. The plum pudding took pride of place in the centre of the old red laminated kitchen table and the red and green ribbon around it gave a small, festive air to the room.

The fridge was on the porch because there was no room in the tiny kitchen for much more than the table and two old mismatched chairs.

Luxury? Huh! She could cope with the décor but wasn't so sure about the outside shower and toilet located at the far end of the back porch. Jilly reached for the salad bag and closed the fridge. The bag crinkled in her hand as she looked down at the unappetizing green leaves. Changing her mind, she pulled open the door again, put the salad back, and pulled out a chocolate bar and a bottle of strawberry milk.

It was Christmas Eve, after all!

This would be her celebratory dinner, and then she'd brave a quick shower outside and have an early night. Look on the bright side; the cottage *was* cutesy in a retro kind of way, although she wondered how secure the back wall of the kitchen was. It was made entirely of latticework and wouldn't keep anything out.

Wind, bugs *or* intruders. And it was swaying in the wind with an ominous creak.

With a deep sigh and a swig of strawberry milk, Jilly searched out a clean towel from the mothball-smelling linen cupboard beside the back door and headed for the shower.

***

Dominic pulled the cap off a bottle of beer and held the cool glass against his forehead. The air was muggy and by the look of the flashing sky and the rumbling to the west there was a decent night storm brewing. He took a swig of the beer, put it on the bench and picked up his keys. He'd clear out the carport and get the Audi under shelter as best he

30

could. There was hail in that sky.

His eyes narrowed as he stepped outside. There was a light on in Derro's cottage down the road. There shouldn't be; no one had lived in their grandparents' place since Derro had died. Aunty Vi had talked about letting it as a holiday rental, but Dominic had convinced her not to. It hadn't taken much talking; as well as the physical problems with the place, the whole family knew the real reason it couldn't be let out.

Not that we ever talk about it.

With a sigh, he shoved his hands in his pockets and hurried down the steps. The last thing he wanted to do was go to the cottage, but he should make sure squatters hadn't moved in. All he wanted was peace and quiet for this break; he didn't want to have to deal with any problems.

Or any other person for that matter. He was here to surf and chill and forget about the cutthroat business world he'd left behind in Sydney.

##

Taking a shower in the tiny cubicle had been

fraught with problems. Jilly had to maneuver an old surfboard out of the small shower recess and brush down the sticky cobwebs that hung from the showerhead to the taps on the wall. No sign of spiders but they could be lurking in the dark. At least the room looked clean, but the smell of moldy concrete pervaded the dimly lit space. She reached up to open the small louvre window at the top of the shower and squealed as a Daddy Long Legs spider scurried across her hand. She shook it off and opted to keep the window half-shut rather than brave the spider and any family he might have.

Slipping her shorts and T-shirt off, she looked around for somewhere to hang her clothes . . . and her towel. Not a hook or a bench to be seen. Opening the door a crack, she shoved them through the gap and placed them on the floor of the verandah, before turning on the taps and waiting. She jumped as another flash of lightning lit the night sky, and a far-off rumble of thunder reverberated along the verandah.

A clanking and groaning preceded the burst of

steaming hot water that sprayed her from above. Jilly jumped back and it took a bit of fiddling to adjust the heat to a comfortable level, but finally she tipped her head back, and closed her eyes, letting the warm water ease her tension.

She was here; the inside of the cottage was clean; the bed was soft, and the beach was a stone's throw across the road. She had food and books to read and a couple of bikinis. What more could she need? This outside bathroom would add to the adventure. She opened her eyes and reached for the shampoo bottle on the floor and tipped it into her hand, lathering her long hair into sweet-smelling suds as a picture of sun-tipped curls came to mind.

What were the chances of running into her boss in a small town so far from Sydney? He was the last person she would ever have expected to see in a pair of boardshorts. She narrowed her eyes as she remembered the sand on the back of his legs. Maybe he wasn't travelling; maybe he was staying in this beachside village although she doubted if there were any flash condos in this town.

Smooth golden skin filled her thoughts as she massaged her hair and imagined massaging those delectable muscles.

Stop it.

No matter how attracted she was to Mr. Dominic Smythe-Phillips, that attraction would be firmly put in its place when she went back to the office. Two work relationships had already gone pear-shaped and Jilly had sworn off them for life. Brad Wallace had used her to get a promotion at the Federal Bank and then suggested she move on when he'd been promoted above her. Luckily, the job at SAB had paid more and given her many more opportunities in the two years she'd been there.

Thanks for the opportunity, *Brad.*

Jilly closed her eyes as she rinsed the suds from her hair.

Phil Long had been worse; there was the wife he'd neglected to mention. Luckily Jilly had found out about her just in time.

So, the new policy she stuck to rigidly: work and sex did not mix. Trouble was, working so hard, and looking after Dad left no time for meeting guys anywhere else.

Celibacy had been the order of her life for a long year.

Creak.

Jilly's eyes flew open as the sound of slow footsteps on the wooden verandah reached her. Quickly rinsing the last of the shampoo from her hair, she switched off the taps and listened. With her heart thudding madly, she opened the door a crack, bent down and reached for the towel. Her hand met smooth, worn floorboards and she stretched her arm out further and patted around the floor. There was no towel beneath her roving fingertips.

Shit. Or clothes. Pulling the door closed quietly, she listened as the front steps creaked.

Great. As she stood there wondering what the hell to do, someone pounded on the back door along the porch. She held her breath; if she was quiet maybe they'd go away. For goodness sake, she was bare-assed naked. When she slowly turned the lock on the inside of the shower door the resulting snick was like a gunshot going off.

So much for trying to keep quiet.

"Hello? Who's there? Where are you?"

"Oh, shit." She'd know that voice anywhere. Jilly rolled her eyes as the deep and sexy voice of Mr. Iceberg drifted through the louvre window.

"Me."

"Who?" His voice was terse now, more like the impatient tones as he queried a report at the office.

"Er . . . I'm in here," she called out.

The footsteps came closer. Jilly leaned against the door and stifled a groan.

Of all the rotten luck.

"Where's here and who's me?" His voice was louder, and she leaned back against the wall and rubbed her arms. The wind was swirling through the gap above the door now and goose bumps rose on her bare, wet skin.

"In the shower." She realized he would have no idea where the shower was. "At the end of the verandah. And it's me, Jilly Henderson."

Silence.

What the hell is he doing here anyway? She stood there shivering as cold rivulets of water ran down from her wet hair to her neck and body. Taking a deep breath, she tried to compose herself. Her nipples gave a little tug before flaring to high beam, ready to say hello to anyone who looked.

Blasted cold.

Jilly had no intention of stepping out of this shower until she had a towel around her and her clothes back from wherever they were.

"Jilly?"

"Yes, it's me."

"What the hell are you doing in there?" The sexy voice had taken on a dangerous edge now. It appeared he was just as unimpressed to find her here, as she was to hear him outside the shower. "I'm taking a shower.

"Why are you here? Did you follow me?"

"Why the hell would I do that?"

If he wanted to play nasty, she could be cranky too. She wasn't at work and she didn't have to put up with his stiff manner like she did most days at work.

37

A tight smile with a muttered good morning was as social and pleasant as he got in the office. Even if he looked sexy when he smiled, he never made friendly overtures to anyone. Hence the Mr. Iceberg tag.

But she was at a disadvantage here.

At least he had clothes on. Well, some clothes anyway. Her nipples tightened as the memory of that golden sun-kissed skin flashed through her mind again.

"Well, what *are* you doing here?"

"I *told* you. I was taking a shower." Her voice was as cold as her skin which was now completely covered with goose bumps. Strange, because the evening was hot and muggy. A cool breeze rushed though the shower and the back of Jilly's neck prickled. A chuckle sounded from the other side of the shower door.

"What's so funny?" Indignation filled her at the thought of Dominic Smythe-Phillips standing outside laughing at her predicament.

Wait a minute. Her eyes narrowed. The only way he would know of her predicament would be if *he'd* moved her clothes and towel.

Another voice came from the other end of the verandah and Jilly strained to hear. There was someone with him. A shiver of fear snaked up her spine.

Don't be stupid, it's only Dominic—the storm was making her skittish.

"Dominic? Look I need some help here." But all she heard was that same quiet chuckle a little closer this time.

"Dominic!" Her voice was shrill as she pushed away the fear that was settling in her chest. There was nothing to be afraid of. This was Dominic Smythe-Phillips, second-in-charge of the largest trading bank in Sydney and a well-respected businessman . . . and her boss. She sat outside his office and spoke to him every day.

Okay, so she didn't know much about him—never a personal conversation—but his quietly spoken demeanor and his rare, albeit sexy, smile told her he was a decent guy. Although he was distant, he was always polite, never lost his temper and had never seemed the sort to play a practical joke.

Like taking my clothes. Another shiver ran down her back and she leaned against the shower wall.

"If you're here, go away. Okay?" Dominic's whisper was quiet and the floorboards on the verandah creaked again.

If you're here? Who else was there?

Jilly looked around the small shower cubicle for something to cover up with but there was nothing there apart from the soap and shampoo bottle.

That would be a great look, she thought. Charge out with a cake of soap over one boob and a bottle of shampoo over the other.

Ta da! Hello Dominic!

A door slammed somewhere outside.

"Just stop it!" His voice was angry now.

"Stop what?" Jilly called out. "Look, I . . . I need a hand in here." *Oh, damn it.* "I . . . I don't mean a hand, I mean I need some help."

"I didn't say that." By the close sound of his voice Dominic was outside the shower now.

"Say what?" It was like some sort of bizarre

40

movie, nothing was making sense, least of all this conversation. "Look, Dominic . . . I mean, Mr. Smythe-Phillips"—keep it formal or as formal as she could, naked and no clothes within reach— "I don't know what you're playing at, but I would be very grateful if you would pass my clothes in."

And then go away.

"What clothes?"

Jilly gritted her teeth. "The clothes and towel you took from outside the shower."

This time she could hear the amusement in his voice. "So, you're in there in your er . . . shall I say . . . in your natural glory?"

So he *could* crack a joke but she was decidedly unimpressed.

"I am in here, waiting for you to return my towel and clothes." Jilly folded her arms across her chest. Her skin was drying rapidly in the cool breeze blowing through the half-open slats of the louvre window. She was not finding this situation the slightest bit amusing, like her boss seemed to be.

"I'm sorry. I don't have them."

41

Jilly couldn't figure out the tone of his voice.

There was another hurried whisper. "I didn't take them.'

"Who else is out there?" She folded her arms.

"No one."

Bullshit.

Another nervous skitter ran up her back. "Well, if you didn't take them can you please find them? A pair of shorts and a T-shirt, and a pink towel." The thought of him finding her undies blowing about the lawn brought heat to her cheeks.

"They must have blown away. There's a nasty storm brewing. I'll go and look down in the yard."

Receding footsteps, soft whispers and then silence. There *was* someone else there with him.

When she'd looked at the Audi at the gas station, Jilly hadn't noticed anyone else with him. But then, she admitted to herself, she'd been too busy perving on his butt to take much notice of anything else. She bit back a groan and reached up to squeeze some of the water from her hair while she waited.

Chapter Four

There was no sign of clothes or a towel on the verandah, or in the long grass at the back of the house. Not that Dominic expected to find them there. He'd felt like an idiot trying to talk to someone who he really didn't believe was there, but Aunty Vi always said—

Shit. Forget about that. He had thought he'd heard a laugh . . . and seen . . . something. Maybe it was just the wind and the moonlight.

His suspicions as to where the clothes had gone were crazy so he wouldn't be sharing them with Jilly Henderson. She'd think he was a total fruit cake if he shared that thought with her. He also wanted to know why the hell she was in Derro's cottage and how long she thought she was staying there. But the way things were shaping up, he suspected she'd be out of there at daylight. Or at least Dominic hoped she would but that created another problem. The town was always booked out from Christmas to mid-January so there'd be no accommodation left.

How the hell had she ended up at the cottage? At the gas station, he'd assumed Jilly would be heading to Byron Bay, or even the Gold Coast. This town was for retirees and surfers; there was nothing sophisticated to do here. And that was how he'd always found her.

Sophisticated and distant. The casually dressed Miss Henderson in the gas station had rocked him.

Dominic came back up the steps and looked around. The breeze had dropped, and the air was still. The chill that had pervaded the verandah a moment ago had gone.

Good.

"Look," he said. "I'm sorry, but I can't find them. The wind must have carried them further than I can see. I can get a torch and go looking further."

"No, thank you. Just go."

"Do you want me to go inside and get you another towel?" He stood outside the door.

"No." The retort was immediate and definite.

"So . . . a nudie run?" The image that flashed though his mind made him want to hang around for the show.

"No!"

Dominic bit back a grin; he wondered what she intended doing. A nudie run would be worth seeing. Her staid black corporate suit had well disguised the lush curves the brief shorts and clinging T-shirt had accentuated. The tightly pulled-back chignon had given no hint to the gorgeous red curls that cascaded down Miss Henderson's back to that delicious rounded butt.

He folded his arms and leaned back on the rail. "So how can I help?"

"Go away and I'll go inside after you've gone."

"No, I want to talk to you."

"Well, talk away."

His lips tilted. This little spitfire was very different to his quiet executive assistant from the office. A southward rush of blood had one part of him very interested.

"How about I go around to the other end of the

verandah, and when you're dressed you can come out and we can talk?"

"How will I know you've gone?" Her voice was wary.

"Because I'm a gentleman and I'm going now. I'll keep my back turned." He pushed away from the railing regretfully. "Promise."

"All right then. No peeking."

"No peeking." Sometimes being a man of his word had its disadvantages, but he wasn't a voyeur. Dominic walked to the end of the verandah and looked across the road to the beach, keeping his back to the small outside bathroom.

The north-easterly wind had picked up and, as dark as it was, he could still see the white caps whipped up out to sea when the lightning flashed. The wind whistled through the trees lining the edge of the road and the first spits of rain landed at the edge of the verandah. He looked up; the clouds were low and scudding fast. If he stayed here much longer, he was in for a soaking on the way home.

A door banged behind him and he turned around

slowly.

He couldn't help the grin as he met the wide-eyed gaze of one very naked woman. One very *beautiful* naked woman. Jilly was tugging on the handle of the back door at the other end of the verandah.

Her eye met his as she dropped her hands to cover herself.

"Turn around," she squealed. "Now!"

Being the gentleman he was—*damn it*—Dominic let the appreciative smile slide as he swung his gaze away.

"The door slammed shut in front of me just as I was about to go in." Indignation seemed to have overcome her embarrassment. Her tone made it sound as though she was holding him responsible.

From the brief glimpse of long, slender limbs and the verification that she was indeed a natural redhead, Dominic wanted to reassure Jilly she certainly had nothing to be embarrassed about. But embarrassment didn't seem to be on the top of her list. Without looking, he could feel the glare she was directing to him. He bit back a smile. His Miss

Henderson was becoming more interesting by the minute.

"Who's here with you?" Her voice was cross now. "Are they inside the cottage?"

"Nobody. I'm here by myself."

"Bullshit." The prim and proper executive assistant *had* long gone. "I heard you talking to someone."

"Uh uh, must have been the wind. There's a fair storm brewing. Look"— Dominic went to turn around and remembered just in time— "you scurry back into the shower, I'll unlock the door, cover my eyes and then you can go inside."

"All right," she said slowly.

"And then we'll talk about *why* you're here."

Five minutes later, things had gone according to his plan. Dominic had managed to get the door open; it hadn't been locked, just jammed shut. He'd dutifully turned his back again while Jilly scurried past. Now she stood at the door dressed in a pair of shorts and a singlet top, her wet curls plastered to the sides of her face. Dominic's fingers itched to reach out and lift the wet strands from her skin, but he didn't think she would appreciate it. Ushering him inside, she pointed to one of the chairs at the old kitchen table—Dominic grinned, the same wooden ones that had been there since he was a kid.

"Now explain." Her voice was short, and her cheeks were flushed. "Did you follow me here?"

He ignored the chair and shook his head. "Where from? Sydney?"

She let out an exasperated sigh. "No, the gas station."

"Why would I do that?" Leaning instead against the old bench top, he folded his arms, watching with fascination as a single droplet of water landed on her shoulder and slowly ran down towards the neckline of her tight T-shirt. "You're the one with the explaining to do, not me. What are *you* doing here? Did you follow me from the gas station?"

"What am I doing here?" Her voice rose with each word. "I'm staying here for my Christmas break."

"No, you're not."

49

"And why would that be, Mr. Smythe-Phillips?" Her voice was laced with saccharine-sweetness and Dominic bit back a smile. If it hadn't been for the fact that she couldn't stay here, he would have quite enjoyed spending a few days getting to know this very different Miss Henderson. This little red-headed kitten was showing her sharp claws and he waited for the reaction which was sure to come when he told her she definitely *wasn't* staying here. He shrugged, putting on a casual air.

"It's my family's cottage and we don't rent it out. You're squatting."

"Squatting!"

"Yep, squatting. How did you get in?"

"With the key!"

"You're still squatting. You'll have to go."

"Be that as it may"—she turned around and picked up a scrunched piece of paper from the table— "this says that I can rent it . . . and I am. I'm not going anywhere. I don't care who owns it. I have a *receipt.*"

Dominic folded his arms and leaned against the

wall ignoring the piece of paper she held out to him.

"No," he said.

Jilly took a step closer to Dominic and eyeballed him. "Yes," she said.

Their eyes met and held; he ignored the little jolt that raced through him as he stared at the golden flecks in her green eyes. They tipped at the corners and were beautiful; he'd never noticed them behind the square, dark spectacles she wore in the office.

"You can't."

"I can."

Mexican standoff. Okay, how could he handle this without looking like a complete fool? Dominic lifted his head as a fleeting shimmer of light flickered briefly. He stared at the wall with a frown and waited for a noise or . . . or something. *He* wasn't used to this yet, so how the hell could he explain it to a stranger?

He shook his head with a frown. It must have been the lightning. If he wasn't careful, he'd end up as crazy as Derro's sister. Thinking quickly, he gathered together the most persuasive argument he could come up with.

"Look, Jilly. Is it okay if I call you that?" He pulled out the best grin he could. "I'm more used to calling you Miss Henderson, but it is the holiday season."

She nodded, hands on hips, chin thrust forward. "You may, Mr. Smythe-Phillips." Despite her belligerent stance, the nod was cool and regal.

So, it was like that was it? She was a tough player in the bank, and it looked like she was going to be as tough to deal with personally.

"I'm really sorry, but you can't stay here. There's been a mistake. This place has been in my family for years and it's in no fit state to be let out. Just take a look around." Dominic ran his hand through his salt-encrusted hair. He'd slipped into town for beer and petrol after he'd been surfing and probably wasn't dressed in a way that would assist his position here as a sort of landlord. "You could get hurt and you could sue us. I don't know how you were able to rent it."

"It was in my staff email. 'Retro holiday cottage on north coast, available to SBA staff only.' I checked it out online, talked to the guy at the phone number

52

given, paid in full by cheque and here I am." She narrowed her eyes as she held the receipt out to him. "To stay."

"What guy? What was his name?" Dominic stared back at her. Her cheeks were flushed.

"Derek somebody."

Bloody hell.

Dominic shook his head slowly. "Look, I don't know how it's happened but there's been a mistake. There is no Derek. You can't stay here. The place is falling down. Look around you. It's in no fit state for guests."

God knew what could happen here during the night. All he knew was, he wouldn't sleep here, and he wasn't about to let a woman—albeit a very attractive woman—sleep here alone. "I'll find you a motel room somewhere."

"No."

"I'll pay for it."

"No."

Dominic should have known the tenacity that had got Jilly Henderson to the position of executive assistant before she was thirty would make her dig her heels in. Yes, he knew how old she was; despite the staff thinking he sat up in some ivory tower, he knew everything there was to know about his executive team. She'd graduated with her MBA a couple of years ago, had recently celebrated her twenty-eighth birthday and lived alone on the lower north shore, not too far from his apartment. As far as he knew she was single; her personal life never intruded on her work at the office and she rarely attended office social functions. His mind ticked over as she stared back at him.

Jilly's shoulders straightened. She walked across to the door and held it open. "Look, Dominic. Is it okay if I call you that?" She parroted his words as she pulled the door open. This time it opened smoothly beneath her hands without the sign of a creak. He stepped through as she ushered him outside with a flick of her hand.

"I'm not a guest, I'm a paying tenant. I don't care about the state of the cottage and don't worry, I won't sue you. I've had a long drive, I'm tired and I want to go to bed." She stepped back and stared at him, obviously waiting for him to leave. "I have no idea why you are here too. However, I do appreciate your concern. Thank you and good night."

Dominic stood on the dark verandah and opened his mouth to speak.

"I'll see you in January," Jilly said.

The door closed in his face.

Chapter Five
Christmas Day

Despite the booming thunder when Jilly finally climbed into bed, she slept soundly and dreamlessly. Mr. Persistent Smythe-Phillips had finally given up trying to persuade her to leave through the closed door.

"If you have any problems through the night—*any*—I'm in the cottage up the road," he said, finally accepting that she was here to stay. "Don't hesitate to call me."

"Don't worry, I'm not the litigious type," she'd called through the door. What a bizarre conversation to be having on Christmas Eve with her boss. She still couldn't believe he was here at this isolated beach.

She had seen a completely different side to him as he had done his best to move her out of the cottage, but she'd stood firm. This was *her* holiday and

56

she wasn't going anywhere unless he could come up with a better reason than the cottage wasn't suitable, according to him.

Dangerous! Pfft. The only dangerous things she'd come across so far were one Daddy Long Legs spider . . . and an altogether too sexy boss.

She shook her head at Dominic being here in this small town. Was it a coincidence? He would have been the last person she'd ever expect to run into in a small beachside village like this. If she'd known the cottage belonged to his family, she would never have rented it. But she had and she was here to stay. Sitting up, Jilly stretched her arms high and looked around. Sunlight was pouring in through the lacy, white nylon curtains at the bedroom window. The storm had died out as she'd drifted off to sleep, snug in the soft bed. The timber walls were painted a soft yellow and the brightness of the room buoyed her mood.

She slid her legs over the side of the bed onto the timber floor. The worn boards were smooth beneath her bare feet as she headed outside to have a wash. A light breakfast, slip into her bikini and sarong, and then hit the beach. A relaxing day of reading and chilling out beckoned.

Time to face her grief and move on. That's what Dad would have wanted her to do. He would have been pleased to know that she'd chosen to spend Christmas here; he could never understand her trips to Bali, Vanuatu and other overseas tropical destinations.

'Look in your own backyard, sweetheart. Our beaches on the north coast are the best in the world.'

Doing what she knew Dad would have approved of, had eased her grief a little. She focused on the happy memories of him teaching her to surf at Narrabeen in the days before life got too hectic to enjoy. When Mum had been alive, and they had been a family.

Tears threatened as she headed for the outside loo. She'd let herself have a good cry one night, and then move on. It was extra tough this year because it was Christmas and she had no family left.

After she'd washed, Jilly stood at the lounge window and had a quick snack of fruit and another full-cream strawberry milk—*sorry hips*—she'd go for a long walk later. The sea air had kicked in and she was hungrier than usual. If she stood on her tiptoes, she could just catch a glimpse of the deep blue water through the she-oaks fringing the sand across the road. Last night's storm had washed everything clean; she pushed the window up and drew in a deep breath of salt-laden air. Peace stole over her and Jilly couldn't help the big grin that crossed her face.

Eight whole days of solitude and bliss ahead—no frantic trading and no emails that must be acted upon immediately.

She put her dishes in the pink porcelain kitchen sink. But although tired and dated, everything in the place was in good condition and clean. She shook her head remembering Dominic's agitation last night. He was worrying about nothing; the cottage was old, but fine. She smiled; it *was* retro in an original sort of way. He could sort out the rental issue with his family; it wasn't her problem.

As she pulled up the bedcovers, something slid from the end of the bed and Jilly bent to pick it up.

She held the unfamiliar plastic bag in her hand and frowned as she turned it over in her hands. She was sure it hadn't been on the bed last night. She opened the bag and peered into it and her frown deepened. The shorts, T-shirt and towel, and undies which she'd assumed had blown off the verandah last night were folded neatly inside.

What the . . .

After Dominic had left, she had gone outside with her torch and searched around the long grass and beneath the low verandah but there'd been no sign of her clothes. How the hell did they get into a bag *and* onto her bed through the night? She put the bag aside and folded her arms, her temper building.

What the hell was he playing at? How *dare* he come into the cottage while she was sleeping? The cottage belonged to his family; he must have another key.

Well, she'd be paying Mr. Smythe-Phillips a visit and telling him to stay away from her. While she was on vacation she didn't have to kowtow to his imperious demands.

##

Jilly detoured via the cottage up the road on her way to the beach. Slipping her beach bag over her shoulder, she passed Dominic's silver Audi. It was parked in a small lean-to on the side of the other cottage. She climbed the stairs identical to the ones at her cottage, took a deep breath and pounded on the front door. This cottage was the same design as the one she was staying in. The same colored paint peeling from the exterior weatherboards and a small bathroom on the far end of the verandah. Her legs were trembling as she practiced her prepared speech. She cleared her throat.

Stay right away from the cottage and from me. The shakiness in her legs, and the funny curling feeling in the pit of her stomach had nothing to do with the anticipation of seeing him again.

No way.

Jilly dug deep to bring back the anger that had coursed through her when she had realized that he had been in her bedroom while she was sleeping.

Ergh. Forget the anticipation that was skittering through her. It was almost creepy; Dominic had certainly conned them at the bank with his gentle and polite manner.

All was silent inside the house, and she pounded on the door again. Perversely, she hoped he was sleeping, and she pounded harder, hoping she'd wake him up. But after a third go of trying to raise the dead with her curled fist on the timber door, all remained silent. Jilly stood there for a moment, biting her lip, before she shrugged and turned away to walk to the beach.

He'd keep till later.

She drew in a gasp of delight as she stepped through the row of she-oaks fringing the sand. Sapphire blue water filled her vision for as far as she could see, and the morning sun sparkled on the water. Snowy-white cumulo-nimbus clouds sat low above the far horizon in the distance, the same color as the foam on the breaking waves that rolled into the beach. The long, lazy swells rolling in across the Pacific steepened and broke into gentle waves as the ocean floor bottomed out, before they pushed up the white sandy shore.

Dad was right. This was one of the most beautiful beaches she'd ever seen. And it was almost deserted.

Far away in the distance, a couple walked ahead of a dog frolicking in the shallows. The rest of the beach was clear, with not another soul in sight. Jilly scanned the sand looking for a spot to settle in for the morning. She'd lathered herself in sunscreen after she'd slipped into her white bikini and had a wide-brimmed hat to protect her face. Her Kindle was charged, and she'd packed two bottles of cold water in her beach bag. She spread her towel on the sand and glanced up as a movement in the water caught her eye. A lone surfer was surfing the point a little to the north. Jilly straightened and put her hand to her eyes with an envious sigh.

Rising gracefully to his feet he turned when his board picked up the front of the wave. He glided effortlessly through the translucent water, so clear she could see the back of the board as he gained speed down the face of the wave. She held her breath as the wave curled over him and he disappeared into the tube for a few seconds before shooting out triumphantly from the right-hand break.

Clapping her hands, Jilly smiled as he turned and paddled back to catch the next wave. It had been a long time since Dad had taught her to surf; she'd spent a lot of time on a board at Narrabeen when she was in her teens. She had never forgotten the power of pushing her board across and down the face of the wave at the same time; the adrenaline rush of the speed combined with the thrill of the movement. Being at one with nature—feeling the air, hearing the whoosh and suck of the wave as water sprayed around you, there was nothing like it.

Lately life had passed her by, and she'd been focused on work and Dad's health, and she'd taken little time for herself.

A good New Year's resolution.

Jilly time 2020!

By the time the surfer caught the next wave she'd settled on her towel and pushed the sand into a mound behind her back to lean on as she read. She narrowed her eyes as the wave pushed him closer to the section of the beach where she was sitting. With a groan, she looked away and picked up her Kindle; she should have known it was Dominic.

But as much as she tried to focus on her book, she couldn't stop looking up and watching as he caught wave after wave in a show of effortless maneuvers. Finally, she gave up and laced her fingers behind the back of her head and gave in to sheer admiration. Who would ever have known that the staid boss of the SAB could carve up a wave like that? He was an absolute pro, as good as any she'd ever watched. A couple of times, Jilly caught her breath as his board teetered on the edge of the wave before he turned and sliced across the face of it. Finally, he caught a wave and paddled to the shore.

She pulled her hat low over her face, quickly picked up her Kindle and rolled over onto her stomach as he walked up the beach. Hopefully he wouldn't notice her on the way back.

Five minutes later, cold water splashed onto the

backs of her legs; her hope had been futile. She rolled over and leaned back on her elbows, squinting up into the bright sunshine.

"Morning, Jilly." Dominic rested his board on the sand and Jilly looked away as he squatted beside her, that golden-tanned chest way too close for her comfort.

"Good morning." She looked away from that magnificent expanse of bare skin, pleased that her sunglasses hid her expression. She pointed to the surf as the next wave crashed onto the beach.

"Pretty impressive surfing."

"You sound surprised." Dominic tipped his head to the side, obviously to clear the water from his ears. Jilly looked up at him as water droplets flew from his wet curls. His eyelashes were salt-encrusted, and his blue eyes were alight with the smile that crossed his face as he stared back at her. His face was tanned, contrasting with the white zinc cream smeared on his nose. He could have passed for an eighteen-year-old; his grin was cheeky, and he looked relaxed and happy.

"I am. It's the last thing I expected to see you

66

doing," she said honestly trying to keep her eyes from his muscled chest. "I'm used to you sitting at a desk in a suit firing orders at me." She flicked a hand towards his board. "Doesn't suit the corporate image I had." Although that image *had* shimmied away last night when she'd seen him in his boardshorts at the gas station.

"You should try it sometime. Nothing like it." He stared out at the sea. "I grew up here and the surf was my life before I left for uni."

Surprise ran through Jilly. She'd always thought he's come from the north shore of Sydney. Silver spoon and all that.

"I know. I love it too." Jilly couldn't help smiling back. "I surfed at Narrabeen when I was at high school."

Dominic grinned at her and her heart did a little flip flop in her chest. She put her hand to her mouth pretending to yawn, forgetting all her previous thoughts of his strange behaviour. The top of his wetsuit had been pulled down and she stared at the glistening water drops on his chest. Despite the bright sun, she could see the frown that suddenly wrinkled his high forehead.

"Did you sleep well?" His tone was probing, and his words jerked her out of that silly adolescent mooning.

"I did. *Unfortunately.*" She killed the smile as it all came flooding back and stared. "And apparently I slept a little too deeply."

"Why?" His voice was cautious. "What do you mean by that?"

"Look, I've calmed down a bit now."

How to put this politely but make her point very clear?

"I went to your cottage to see you on the way here and I was pretty angry."

"Because?"

"Because I don't appreciate you just letting yourself into my cottage whenever you feel like it. I don't care if the place belongs to your family. If it happens again, I'll—"

"Whoa. Just wait one minute. You think I was there while you were asleep? That's sick. No way did I—or would I ever do that."

His expression and the horrified indignation in his tone convinced her immediately he was telling the truth.

"Well, who else would put my clothes into a plastic bag and leave them on the end of my bed? Do you provide a maid service in your holiday rentals?" Her tone was sarcastic, but she wanted an answer. If he hadn't put them there, who had?

"Trust me." Dominic stared at her and his voice was soft. He balanced on the balls of his feet and looked away from her out to the sea as he ran his hand through his hair. "I believe you, but I just want you to know that I did not—and would not—come into your cottage uninvited. It wasn't me. My cousin, Margaret, has a key. Maybe she found them?"

Jilly pushed herself to her feet and brushed the loose sand from her legs. He'd been too close for her comfort in the sand beside her. "Okay, if you say so, I guess I'll take your word for it."

He stood and she tipped her head to the side and looked at him curiously. Even though he had denied it and she had no reason not to believe him, he still looked ill at ease.

"Okay, if it wasn't your cousin, maybe I just had a memory lapse or something." She reached out to touch his arm in an attempt to lighten the tension. "I've had a tough few days and I'm pretty tired. I really needed this break. My boss works me very hard, you know." She let a tentative smile cross her face. He looked so concerned she felt bad.

"Thank you." Dominic straightened his shoulders and Jilly had to tip her head back to keep eye contact. "Have you given any more thought about moving to a motel?"

Jilly put her hands on her hips and jutted her chin out as any sympathy fled.

"No."

Chapter Six

Dominic looked down at the woman staring at him. He knew very well how hard Jilly Henderson worked, and he was just sorry that the chances of her having a restful Christmas in that cottage were slim. He stared down at her beautiful green eyes as they locked with his. A man could drown in them. He'd not been immune to her at the office, but he had tried to ignore it. Even though she was quiet and professional in her dealings with him, he'd often heard her laughter coming from the morning tea room as she'd chatted to the other staff. But she'd always kept a barrier up between them and it had rankled, even though avoiding office romances was a policy he'd stuck to religiously as he'd climbed the corporate pole. Too many issues in the business world were generated by office relationships after a fling. Friday night staff drinks were notorious for beginning relationships between staff that were

71

committed elsewhere.

And it always happened at this time of the year; another reason to avoid the Christmas drinks that seemed to be on every night from the first of December until the big office party when there was inevitably a tale of woe. Staff turnover from the Christmas party fallout was a given every year.

But not for him.

"Earth to Dominic." Jilly's familiar voice washed over him. He ignored the little jolt that headed for his groin but was thankful that he was wearing boardshorts over his budgie smugglers. The budgie had already given a little chirp when Jilly's hand had touched his arm a moment ago.

"Sorry. You had me back in the office for a while there. And yes, I do know how hard you work." He wasn't going to mention someone being in in her cottage—if she was prepared to put it down to a memory lapse, he wasn't going to discourage it. But he was going to do his damnedest to make sure it didn't happen again.

If I had a bloody clue how to, that is.

"So, seeing your boss is such a hard taskmaster, he needs to make sure you have a great holiday. How would you like to come for a surf with me in the morning?" Dominic couldn't take his eyes off Jilly when her face broke into a wide smile. She was drop dead *gorgeous*. And if he kept his eyes on her face, his gaze wasn't tempted to stray to the luscious curves packaged in that white bikini.

"Oh, yes please! That'd be awesome. Do you have a spare board?"

"I do, but I'm pretty sure we'll find a smaller one to suit you in the shed at the back of your cottage. It shouldn't be locked. I'll come down and have a look this afternoon if that's okay?" He waited for her nod. After last night's antics, he wasn't going to go near the place and give her any reason to doubt him. As far as he knew all his and Derro's boards had been there for years. He was the only one of all the cousins who ever came back to the coast. Except for Margaret; she'd never moved away. The rest of them were scattered far and wide over the world in a variety of careers. One thing he could say about the Smythe-

Phillips; they were all high achievers.

Except for Derro, but maybe he'd known what life was going to hold for him.

Dominic gazed out over the ocean; Derro had never had a career goal. Surfing had been his life and it had caused his death before he was twenty. His ashes had been scattered to the wind on this very beach ten years ago. Guilt ran through him; he hadn't caught up with Margaret for years. She'd been the older, crazy cousin as they'd grown up and run wild at their grandparents' beach cottages and Derro's death had tipped her into eccentricity. When he'd last seen her, he'd been shocked at how much she'd aged.

Despite the sadness that came with being here, Dominic had looked forward to coming home. This was the place he could be himself and not the corporate suit that he'd turned into. He had planned to use this week as a time to reconsider his future. His current life was not what he wanted for himself, even if he was making a success of it. Maybe it was time for a change; a sea change. Even after only two nights away from Sydney, peace was stealing through his bones. But he certainly didn't need the complication of anyone in that cottage and the problems it could bring.

That person was now staring up at him with a strange expression on her face.

Jilly reached out again and touched his arm gently. "Dominic?"

"Yes?" He gave his head a gentle shake. She had a terrible effect on him; his thoughts were all over the place.

"Merry Christmas."

"Oh. I forgot. And to you too." A chuckle accompanied his words. "How about when I come over, I bring a couple of beers and we can sit on your porch and watch the storm after we dig out a board for you?" He'd had no intention of saying that and his words surprised him. At least if he was there, he could keep her safe. Not that he thought she could really come to any harm. After all what could—

"Storm?" Jilly frowned at him and lifted her eyes to the clear blue sky.

"Guaranteed to be a storm later." Dominic lifted

his head and sniffed the pure air. "Can't you smell it?"

Jilly's pretty laugh trilled around him. "No, I can't, but I'll take your word for it. And yes, it would be nice to have some company."

Despite her laugh, he was surprised to see a tear drop from the tip of her long eyelashes. He reached out and used the pad of his thumb to wipe it from her cheek.

"You okay?"

She let out an unladylike sniff and wiped her hand over her eyes. "Sorry. First Christmas without my dad. I thought I'd be okay, but I guess I'm not."

"Nothing to be sorry about. It's tough, isn't it? What about your mum?"

Jilly shook her head mutely.

He stared over her head to the ocean and let her gather herself together.

"I lost both my parents in the same year. It's hard. Times like Christmas and birthdays really bring it home," he said.

"Come on over later. When you're ready." A small smile tilted her lips. "I'll try not to be rude to you this afternoon.'

Dominic picked up his board and hitched it beneath his arm. He was reluctant to go back to the cottage; he was enjoying her company. "Okay, sounds like a plan; I'll see you later." As he turned away, Dominic allowed himself one lingering glance at the lush curves in the white bikini.

Yep, she's drop-dead gorgeous.

Maybe his office rule could take a break too.

Chapter Seven

Jilly didn't spend much longer on the beach; the summer sunshine was burning hot. With her fair skin, she'd end up looking like a lobster. It took her a while to get immersed in her book; the sight of Dominic walking away from her with the board beneath his arm, his strong muscles flexing, had set her heart in a little pitter patter, and it was hard to concentrate. Then she opened her Kindle and tried to focus on one of the romances she had downloaded. For a couple of hours, she buried herself in an imaginary world, not giving any thought to Dominic or the sorting out of Dad's stuff that waited for her back in Sydney.

Eventually, the hot sun—not to mention the steamy scenes in the romance—got too much and she packed up her bag and towel. The sexy romance about a holiday fling had her thoughts heading in an inappropriate direction.

A holiday fling? *Maybe that's what I need?*

Uh, uh. She shook her head. Not with her boss. Although it *was* becoming harder to reconcile the Dominic of the surf with Mr. Smythe-Phillips of the office. Maybe it would help if he put a shirt on. Too much naked chest for her comfort.

But what a gorgeous naked chest.

Jilly grinned as she headed back to the beach house. She paused as she opened the gate to the path that led to the front door. Someone had mowed the grass and cleaned up the garden while she'd been at the beach. The cottage looked prettier with smooth, green lawn surrounding it; more like the photo in the email. The edges had been trimmed and the long grass outside the fence was neatly clipped too. She closed the gate behind her and took two steps before she stopped dead and looked around slowly, her mouth dropping open.

Her car was gone. Jilly spun on her heel and looked back to the road; no sign of it. She climbed the steps slowly and walked along the verandah to the door and her heart lodged in her throat. The door was wide open and the key she had locked it with was in her beach bag. She put her bag on the table outside the door and poked her head inside cautiously.

"Hello?" Her voice was husky, and she cleared her throat. "Dominic? Are you in there?" Her eyes settled on the small dining table. Her car keys were sitting exactly where she had left them last night. But a small vase filled with pretty summer flowers was in the middle of the table.

Jilly frowned and backed out through the doorway before walking to the far end of the verandah and peering around the back of the house. She let out the breath she had been holding. Her little red sedan was parked behind the shed in the longer grass. Whoever had mowed had moved her car to the back. Folding her arms, she marched along the verandah and stepped back inside.

Thoughtful, but presumptuous.

"Is there anybody here?" Her temper was growing by the minute. If Dominic had wanted her to move her car so he could mow, all he'd had to do was ask. God, he knew she was on the beach; he could have waited till she came back.

How dare he just walk in, pick up her keys and move her car as though he owned the place? Well, in a way, he did. The place belonged to his family, but she was a tenant and she didn't feel at all comfortable with him having free access to where she was staying. She was tempted to march up and front him straight away, but she'd wait until he came down later.

Jilly picked up her Kindle, raided the fridge for a healthy snack and wandered back outside. She narrowed her eyes. In between the door and the shower halfway along the verandah, a small hammock chair hung from a hook. She walked up to it and gave it a gentle push as she looked around. She was sure that chair hadn't been there last night when she'd had her shower. She shrugged; it looked inviting, calico macramé knots held it together and colorful cushions invited her to sink in and curl her legs up.

Jilly backed into the hammock and sat cross-legged, testing the weight, before she leaned back against the soft cushions.

Okay, putting up a chair like this for her to chill

81

in, maybe she could forgive him for coming by while she was at the beach. It *was* thoughtful to mow the lawn and move her car, so it didn't get chipped. Maybe he was just trying to make amends for being so insistent that she move to a motel.

Not a chance. She could see herself spending the rest of the week rocking in this chair reading. Putting one foot against the wooden rail at the edge of the verandah, she pushed hard, and the hammock rocked gently from side to side.

Bliss. Just what she needed.

Jilly flipped open the Kindle and began to read. She took a deep breath as the sexy scenes got hotter and hotter.

Oh, my.

She read until her eyelids began to droop, keen to keep reading as the story came to a searing climax. Finally, she put her Kindle aside and snuggled into the cushions for an afternoon nap. The only problem with the hammock was it wouldn't swing unless you pushed it, but Jilly was too comfy and she closed her eyes and let sleep overtake her.

##

Creak, creak, creak. The gentle swinging of the hammock chair soothed Jilly as she surfaced from the delicious realms of sleep a while later. She stretched and rubbed her eyes as the chair rocked from side to side; she'd had the most explicit dream about Dominic. A smile crossed her face; that's what she got for reading steamy romance novels. As she came fully awake, she stiffened. The chair was swinging from side to side as someone pushed it from behind.

God, I dream about him and he turns up.

"Dominic?"

No reply. The hammock swung away, and she had to hang onto the side to avoid falling out.

"That's so not funny." Jilly waited until the swinging slowed and putting her feet to the ground, she slid out of the chair. She really wasn't appreciating her boss's sense of humor. Putting her hands on her hips, she opened her mouth and stepped to the back of the chair. Goose bumps pricked her arms and the hair on the back of her neck rose as a coldness swept along the verandah.

83

There was nobody there. The chair was rocking by itself. Jilly closed her mouth and put her hand on the chair to stop it swinging. Deep in thought, she walked to the end of the small porch and looked up the road. There was no sign of anyone. The sky was clouding over but the air outside was still with the expectant hush before a storm. There was no birdsong and only the sound of the gentle whoosh of the waves breaking on the sand reached her.

It must have been the wind.

But there is none.

Maybe she'd done it herself as she'd been waking up?

Jilly turned as the silence was broken by the purr of a motor and Dominic's silver Audi cruised past. He lifted his arm in a wave but kept driving to his house further up the road.

***

Dominic narrowed his eyes as he waved to Jilly. The garden around the cottage had been cleaned up and the lawn mown.

Nice of her to do that. He'd intended offering to do it tomorrow, but she'd obviously found the old push mower in the shed while he'd been in town getting some snacks; he had a few beers in the fridge. Luckily the gas station where he'd run into her last night had opened for a few hours on the public holiday, and it had been deserted today. He drove into the small covered lean-to shed. The sky to the southwest was black with tinges of green with the promise of hail. They were in for a pearler of a storm this afternoon.

After taking a quick shower, he grabbed the six-pack of beer from the fridge and sauntered down the road. Anticipation filled him at the prospect of spending some time with Jilly.

Maybe getting to know her a bit better. He could hear the shower running on the verandah and he looked up as he crossed the newly-mown grass. A pink towel was hanging on the hook outside the door.

Good. No funny business this afternoon. Keep it that way.

Dominic put the beer on the table and walked down the stairs toward the back shed to see if their old boards were still in there. A grin crossed his face as Jilly's out of tune voice followed him down the steps as she sang in the shower.

Shake your booty? The picture that came to his mind kept the grin on his face. He'd never be able to look at Miss Henderson across the boardroom table again without thinking of her in a white bikini and shaking *her* booty.

Maybe he needed another cold shower. He'd turned the water down as cold as he could after he'd got back from the beach this morning, but it hadn't damped down the desire that had heated his blood since last night.

Opening the door of the old shed, he pushed aside the cobwebs and poked around until he came across the old kneeboards in the rafters. Still in their cloth bags and secured safely for ten years.

Good on you, Derro.

Dominic lifted the dark green board down—that one had been his favourite when he'd been learning to surf—and carried it up to the verandah; it was waxed ready to go. Strange that the wax hadn't dried up; must have been a good brand.

The singing had been replaced by a muttering and a strange rattling noise.

"Jilly? Are you okay?"

"No, I'm not. What the *fu* . . . what the heck are you playing at?"

He hurried along the verandah to the shower. The pink towel was still hanging on the hook. "Are you still in the shower?"

"Of course, I am. Now unlock the door and stop playing silly buggers."

Dominic stood outside the shower and rolled his eyes. The bolt high on the outside of the shower door was drawn, effectively locking her in.

How am I going to explain that?

"Heh heh." The soft chuckle came from behind him and Dominic whirled around but of course there was nobody there.

"Stop laughing and unlock the door." Jilly was very unimpressed if the tone of her voice was any indication. He'd heard that exact tone when she'd been on the phone to the trading floor each time the share market fell.

He reached and up and slid the bolt open. "It's unlocked now, but Jilly, I swear I didn't lock it."

"So who did?"

"It must have jiggled its way along when you were singing?"

Dead silence.

"Go away, until I get out of here." Her voice was a bit softer. "Please, just go for a walk or something."

The door pushed open slowly and Dominic took off back to the shed. He would do as instructed.

Jilly's turn to be the boss.

Chapter Eight

After she dried off in the bedroom, Jilly pulled on a clean pair of shorts and singlet top before she tied her purple sarong in a fancy twist around her neck, so it looked like a dress. Her temper was simmering; she was very unimpressed with Dominic's juvenile antics.

What was his problem? Nice to her face, and offering to take her for a surf?

Have a chat? Have a beer together? And then play stupid pranks on her?

So different to her serious boss from work. She shrugged before she ran a brush though her hair and twisted it up in a clip. He could come clean about the silly practical joke and they could laugh about it. All she wanted was honesty.

Staring at herself in the mirror, she frowned. If she was honest, she had to admit that the sight of Dominic was making her want more than that.

She ran a smudge of lip gloss across her lips

89

before she stepped outside. He was at the far end of the porch watching the clouds swirl above the beach. The storm was building from the south and lightning lit the late afternoon sky. He turned as she walked along the wooden floor, her bare feet silent on the timber.

Jilly stood in front of him with her arms folded. He could talk first and explain what he was up to. He smiled but didn't speak.

She couldn't help herself. "So?"

The smile got wider, and irritation buzzed through her.

"So what?" he said. Was this guy really second-in-charge of a multi-billion-dollar trading bank?

"So what's with the teenage boy pranks? And while I'm saying my piece, I thought you'd agreed last night to stay out of my cottage while I was here."

This time Dominic frowned back at her. "What do you mean? I haven't been here today . . . not until now anyway. What pranks?"

"Like mow the lawn? And move my car?" Jilly leaned back against the verandah rail while she waited

90

for him to answer, but all she got was a shake of his head. "And push my chair?" Her voice was softer now because she knew he couldn't have done that. He'd driven past a few seconds later.

He seemed to be thinking for a moment and Jilly narrowed her eyes waiting for his latest excuse.

"No. I've been in town."

"So who mowed the lawn?"

He shrugged. "My aunt organizes the upkeep of the place. The handyman must have come while we were at the beach."

"On Christmas Day?"

He shrugged. "This is the north coast, not the city."

Her temper eased a little. "So, you didn't move my car and leave the house door open?"

"No. I didn't, and I wouldn't do that without checking with you." He smiled at her and the crinkles around his eyes made him look even sexier.

"Okay then . . . and you say the shower locked itself." Just as well he'd been here to get her out because there was no one else within calling distance and she would have been stuck in there.

"I'll have to prop it open next time I have a shower."

"I can hang around if you want to lock it." Dominic ran his hand through his hair and stared at her. Jilly's gaze dropped to his lips and a warm tremor ran though her as she remembered the dream she'd had about him. Followed instantly by heat flooding her cheeks.

He screwed his face up into a strange expression, opened his mouth, shook his head and then closed his mouth again. Jilly had never seen this confident man at a loss before. Finally, he ran his hand through his hair. "You *can't* stay here. I'm not going to say anymore because I don't want you to think I'm batshit crazy but—"

She waited for him to finish but Dominic held out his hand. "Come on. That beer's getting warm. We are going to have a Christmas drink and you can tell me a bit about yourself. Why you came up here for a holiday."

Jilly hesitated and then reached out and took his

hand. Pleasant warmth tingled up her arm and headed south as he led her to the outdoor table and pulled out the chair. He popped the top of a beer and passed it to her, and she tipped it to her mouth, appreciating the cold liquid. The beer soothed her parched throat but the effect of one drink zinged through her whole body. She peeped from beneath half-closed lids as Dominic lifted his bottle, but he was looking at her. His gaze travelled slowly over her bare shoulders, down to the knot where her sarong was tied. It had been a long time since anyone had looked at her like that and a small thrill ran through her. She took another sip of beer; she needed to do something to ignore the rapid beat of her heat. She knew a flirtatious look; it might have been a long time between drinks, but she could read his mind.

"Not quite the Hilton where the firm held the Christmas drinks." He smiled as she leaned back on the padded vinyl chair that was beneath the scarred wooden table. "I didn't see you there?"

A bolt of grief shot up from her chest and lodged in her throat. Jilly looked down at the table.

The pre-Christmas function had been the same day as Dad's funeral. The girls couldn't understand why she wouldn't go, but she'd told no one about her Dad until she'd come back to work the day after the funeral. Finally, she lifted her head. "I was at a . . . a . . . funeral. I wasn't being anti-social."

"I'm sorry to hear that."

She lifted her head and he was looking curiously at her.

"You didn't miss much. A lot of silliness, too much drinking and some sore heads the next day."

"I heard how Shaz got Mr. Burns up on the dance floor.' She let out a little giggle. "Apparently he can tango with the best of them."

The ache in her throat eased as a sweet smile crossed Dominic's face. "The rose she put between his teeth was a nice touch."

"She's a mad character. Lightens the place up, doesn't she?" She was a good friend to Jilly, but despite that, Jilly didn't share much personal stuff with any of her work friends.

"She is. I often wonder why people let their hair

down at work functions."

Jilly shrugged. "I know what you mean. Everyone is formal and on their best behaviour all year, and one night in the festive season can bring it all undone." She smiled at him ruefully. "And there speaks the voice of experience."

It was at last year's Christmas party that she'd met Phil's wife. That had been the last social work function she'd been to.

"You too?" Sympathy filled his expression. "I learned very early that work and pleasure don't mix." This time his laugh was rueful. "About ten years back, in my first position as a trader at the Federal Bank, I discovered too late that the lady who had me bailed up under the mistletoe was the chairman's wife."

Jilly relaxed as her laugh bubbled up. "I didn't know you worked at the Federal Bank."

He laughed with her. "I didn't after that. She told him I'd approached her!"

A serious note crept into her voice. "I worked there for a while too. It was an office romance that brought me undone too."

Dominic lifted his beer in the air. "Merry Christmas, Jilly. Here's to no office romances."

She lifted her beer and clinked the glass against his, ignoring the pang of regret that ran through her.

Dominic reached down to a bag on the floor. "I almost forgot. I brought some dinner. Courtesy of the gas station." He pulled out a tin of smoked oysters, and some crackers and cheese. "I was going to suggest maybe cooking some steaks on the barbie, but the weather's put a stop to that."

Jilly uncurled her legs from beneath her and stood before disappearing into the kitchen. "I'll be back in a minute."

The smile that crossed Dominic's face when she put the plum pudding and custard in the middle of the table made the wait in the supermarket car park well worth it.

Thanks, Ethel.

"Merry Christmas to you too."

She sat back down and picked up her beer and watched as he traced his fingers over a scratch in the middle of the table. She leaned forward; DSP was scratched into the wood.

"So, you spent time here when you were growing up?" Jilly watched as his fingers moved across to another scratch. "Family house, you said?"

He looked up and held her eyes with his. "More than that. After my parents died, I grew up here at my grandparents' house. The one up the road where I'm staying. This one was Aunty Vi's." He jerked his head to the side. "Lived there till I left for uni."

"You?" Jilly pointed to the other initials near his. "Sisters and brothers?

"No, just me and my cousins." He picked up the oysters and peeled back the lid. "Two of them lived here and the other cousins who lived in Brisbane used to come and visit once a year. Christmas here was a busy and noisy time."

"Where are they all now?"

"Mostly scattered all over the world. And my grandparents passed on."

"I just lost my Dad." The words were out before she could think.

"So that's why you took some time off?"

She nodded mutely as the grief resurfaced.

"You should have taken longer." The kindness in his voice almost brought her undone and Jilly swallowed and changed the subject.

"It was what? Three days?" His gaze was fixed on her and she dropped her lashes and ran her finger around the rim of the bottle.

"Yeah, it was long enough. It's okay. But I might need the odd day to sort out the estate when we go back." Jilly sat back in her chair as he arranged the oysters next to the crackers and then passed the plate to her. "Thank you. And here I was thinking you were a city boy. Private school, old boys' network and all that."

He looked at her quizzically over his beer.

"Shouldn't make assumptions, should I?" She lifted her beer and closed her eyes as she drank.

"What about you?"

"Guilty," she said. "Private school, uni and Dad's old boys' network got me the job at the bank."

"Everything you thought I was," he said with a quizzical look.

She nodded guiltily.

A comfortable silence settled between them and they sat back watching the storm come in over the sea. Jilly glanced at Dominic as he tipped his beer back and drank. He was wearing a shirt with the sleeves cut out. When he lifted his beer to his mouth, the muscles in his upper arm moved and Jilly couldn't help staring.

For someone who spends all day in the office he looks pretty damn hot.

A shaft of raw desire ran through her and she forced herself to look away, but not before she caught his gaze. Sweat dampened her brow and the skinny tank top she'd changed into after her shower clung to her chest. She looked down dismayed to see her nipples hard beneath the shirt. Lifting her eyes, heat ran through her; Dominic's eyes were at the same spot. She focused her attention on his lips. She'd never noticed how lush and kissable they were.

Jilly averted her eyes as she let out a shaky breath. For a moment, she'd thought he was going to lean over and kiss her. And it wouldn't have been unwelcome. Tension hovered in the air until he reached over and put his hand on top of hers on the table.

"Jilly—" The moment was broken as a sudden wind roared in from the ocean, accompanied by a loud crack of thunder. The hammock chair began to rock back and forth creaking loudly, and the shower door blew shut and the bolt slid across. The tension dissipated in a moment. They looked at each other and smiled.

"See, these things happen." Dominic stood and walked over to the shower and opened the lock. "All you need now is to find the person who mowed the lawn and I'm out of trouble." Those sexy lips opened in a wide grin and his white teeth flashed in the dimness that had descended as the black clouds raced in.

"I'll have to be more careful from now on." Jilly stood and walked across to the railing where he was leaning looking out to the storm. "I'm sorry. I do seem to be blaming you for everything that goes wrong." A low chuckle reached her, and she turned around with a frown. "What was that?"

"What?" Dominic looked around.

"That noise. Did you laugh?' The hair on Jilly's neck stood to attention again—as did her nipples. Not that they'd ever gone down. She rubbed her arms, making out she was cold, nothing to do with this sexual attraction that was consuming her. As she let her gaze move up past those muscled arms to his sexy lips, she wondered how the hell she'd ever work next to him without combusting into a haze of lust.

He was just too damned good looking.

"Are you scared here by yourself?" Dominic leaned in closer to her and she got a whiff of surf, and sand, and sweaty man. She couldn't help taking a deep breath and inhaling the manly essence.

"No, why would you ask that?"

He shrugged. "It's pretty lonely out here. For a city girl."

"I'm fine. I'm enjoying the quiet." Jilly wasn't going to let him know how unsettled she was. It was only the storm that was bothering her. Not him or the spooky feeling that wouldn't go away. The old cottage took on a sinister air as more lightning flashed in from the sea.

"Are you still up for a surf in the morning?" Dominic pointed to the board propped up against the wall. "I found my old kneeboard in the shed. It's all waxed and ready to go."

"Will the weather be okay?"

"Guaranteed. This is just a summer storm." Like the tumultuous feelings that were coursing through her as the touch of his hand warmed her skin. Her body was reacting to him with surprising heat. She lifted her drink and drained the beer, welcoming the fizz that coursed through her blood.

"For sure."

Another chuckle came from the dark and despite the heat of Dominic's body beside hers, goose bumps rose on her skin.

"Who was that?"

"Just the wind. Don't be nervous." His arm went around her, and he squeezed her shoulder and Jilly put aside her jumpiness.

Grow up, she chastised herself. He was right; this

was a very different place to her apartment in Manly where there were people around day and night.

She swallowed as he kept his arm there; he was flirting with her and she didn't mind one bit. They weren't at work now; it was a vacation. Maybe she could put her rules aside for a day or two.

"I hope the weather's okay for our surf tomorrow. I'm looking forward to it." She shivered as the wind whipped around the verandah. "Do you want to come inside before this rain hits."

The cold breeze chilled her skin as Dominic stepped away. "It's time I went home." He'd put a barrier up suddenly. And his expression was back to that of Dominic, the boss. Was she giving out vibes he didn't want?

Jilly shrugged as she took a step back. Literally and emotionally. "What about the plum pudding?"

"Let's save it for after our surf tomorrow. You think I work you hard in the office, you ain't seen nothing yet. We'll get you working those waves." The distance had left his voice, but he moved towards the steps.

"Thanks for the beer. Do you want to take the rest back with you?"

"Nah." He waved dismissively. "Put them in your fridge. New Year's Eve is coming up."

"What time in the morning?" She kept her voice casual not wanting him to see her disappointment.

"Sunrise too early? Meet me on the beach."

Jilly nodded and with a final wave, Dominic disappeared into the darkness and emptiness surrounded her.

Chapter Nine
Boxing Day

Despite the unsettled feeling that wouldn't leave Jilly as she sat on the lounge and read after a light dinner, she slept well. Before she went to bed, she double checked the locks on the window and the doors and left a light on in the kitchen. There was nothing she could do about the thin piece of lattice at the back of the kitchen that shook in the wind. She still couldn't shake the feeling that someone was watching her, which she knew was stupid, because there was no one within cooee.

Apart from Dominic. But one minute, he'd been up close and personal and then he'd withdrawn into himself and left in a matter of minutes.

The alarm on her iPhone roused her at 4.30 a.m. and she stumbled into the kitchen, rubbing her eyes, and reached for the kettle. Her hand froze on the tap as she looked up at the back door. *Unlocked and wide open*. And not only that, the surfboard that Dominic had left outside on the verandah was lying along the sofa, the cotton draw string bag that had encased it, lay scrunched on the rose-covered mat.

Jilly backed away and looked around.

"What the hell?" Her hands shook as she shut the back door and flicked the lock over. She'd forget about the cup of tea; just get changed and head to the beach.

Get out of this house. Forget about what Dominic said about it not being safe, being in here was beginning to creep her out a little.

The first rosy glimmers of dawn were streaking the sky with a soft apricot when she stepped outside, the board tucked beneath her arm. A warm wind puffed in off the hills this morning and everything had been washed clean from the storm last night. The wind must have blown the door opened, she reasoned to herself. And she must have carried the board inside when she was half-asleep and forgotten that she had. If she wasn't careful, she was going to have herself spooked and head home early, which she really didn't want to do. Sydney would be hot and busy, and she'd probably end up at work if she went home early.

Dominic tried to tell you not to stay here, a little voice nagged within her.

He was waiting for her on the beach, his strong, muscular lines silhouetted by the rising sun behind him. The wet sand was smooth and shining, clear of footprints, as Jilly followed him to the water's edge.

"Sleep okay?" His eyes were hooded.

"Like a baby."

Well, I did.

"Good. Surf's great. You ready?" He waited for her to catch him up and they walked out into the water together until they were waist-deep. They waited for a break in the waves. When the last wave of the set broke and passed them with the white frothy foam bubbling around them, Dominic slid onto his board and lay on his stomach and began to paddle out into the deeper water. Anticipation filled Jilly as she waited for the next wave to pass. The rough wax on the board crumbled beneath her fingers as she gripped the sides with both hands and slid onto the length of the board. Before she could find her centre of balance, her bare stomach slid along the slippery board and she held on tight as the board slid away.

It was too late. The board bucked beneath her as the oncoming wave lifted the front of it and Jilly slipped off. She wasn't quick enough and gasped, copping a mouthful of saltwater as she went under the small wave that broke over her, and then carried the kneeboard into the shore.

It was a tossup whether embarrassment or temper won out, and she let her temper build. That was the final straw. What the hell was Dominic playing at? Coughing and spluttering, she marched back through the shallows—as much as one could march in knee-deep water and stood at the edge of the sand, her arms folded as she waited for him to catch the next wave into shore.

Of course he did it gracefully, staying on the board until he was in knee-deep water.

"Are you okay? What happened?" He tossed his head back and his hair stuck to his neck. He reached up and brushed the long strands from his eyes.

Jilly glared up at him. "Just what is your problem? Do you really have to go to these extremes to get me to move out of your precious cottage? I suppose it was you who came back and left the door open last night when you brought the board inside, too?" Her words ran together as rage filled her chest.

The water splashed around Dominic's legs as he strode from the water. His mouth was tight, and his eyes were flashing as he put his board down carefully on the sand and turned to her.

"Would you like to tell me exactly how it's my fault that you fell off your board? I thought you said you could surf?"

Jilly let her temper burn ever hotter. She didn't have red hair for nothing. She picked up the board and shoved it at him "When did you do that? In the middle of the night when I was asleep? You really do have a problem, don't you?"

Socializing and being pleasant to her boss was no longer an option after this prank. How the hell she was going to take him seriously enough to work with from now on was something she'd worry about when she went back to Sydney.

"I need this break and I'm not going to let you, or anyone else ruin it for me!"

She turned away, intending to leave him there, but stopped when Dominic reached out and held her arm. He held her firmly and took her board with his free hand. She saw the exact moment that he realized what she was upset about.

"Bloody hell," he said.

"Is that all you've got to say?" Jilly pulled her arm away and folded her arms. "Why on earth would you put soap on my board instead of wax?"

He put the board down on the ground and turned to her, his other hand holding her shoulder lightly. "I didn't." His eyes narrowed as he stared down at her. "And what was that you said about the door being open?"

"Don't worry about it. I'm going to go back, have a shower—and leave the door propped open while I have it—and have a peaceful day away from you." She lifted her chin and held his gaze with hers.

"So, are you going to let me go?"

Damn him. No matter how angry she was, Jilly had to admit how he really was irresistible. In a suit he'd looked fine, but standing in front of her, sun-drenched muscles, golden-chested and dripping with salt water, he was ridiculously handsome. Like some Greek god or something. She couldn't bear to think how much better he'd look without anything on at all. She blinked as she tried to clear the picture and the stupid comparisons from her mind. What the heck was wrong with her?

His chuckle was husky as he looked down at her. "I'm so sorry. I should have checked the board better." He reached up and tucked her hair behind her ear. "I'm really sorry. I'll stay out and you can have my board. I'll go back and get some wax."

Jilly shook her head, bemused as his eyes held hers. His touch was sending trembles down her back. "So who soaped the board?"

Dominic stared down at her, his expression unreadable. "My cousin used to do it for a lark. He was the world's biggest practical joker."

Jilly picked up the sadness in Dominic's voice. "Was?" she asked quietly.

He lifted his gaze and pointed to the rocks on the point to the south. "Derro drowned on the point the day after his eighteenth birthday."

Chapter Ten

Jilly's lips parted in sympathy as Dominic told her about Derro. He'd not spoken of the tragedy for years and his voice caught as he told her of waiting on the beach that afternoon; waiting hopelessly for Derro to reappear after he'd slipped beneath the water. But he hadn't.

"Luckily I had my phone and I called triple zero. The guys from the surf club in the next bay were here on the jet ski within minutes." He shook his head and lifted his gaze to the horizon. "It took two days for his body to wash up. His sister, Margaret found him. It was a pretty tough time for our family."

Jilly reached over and squeezed his hand. Dominic curled his fingers around hers and didn't let go.

They sat on the sand together as the sun climbed quickly in the morning sky. He didn't tell her what was in his head, or a feeling within his heart; he had no proof and he didn't want to sound crazy.

113

"This is the first time I've had that board out since then, and he obviously had the last laugh. I suppose the soap dried up and as soon as it hit the water, it got slippery."

Last night he'd pulled back when she'd mentioned going inside. He knew she was attracted to him and he'd run. It was all too complicated; being her boss and the crazy situation at the beach cottage that he still couldn't get a handle on.

The sun caught her beautiful green eyes as she turned to him. His confusion dissipated like the spray above the waves as she steadily held his gaze. Instead of pulling away as he expected, she reached up and cupped his jaw in her hand.

"Forget about the board. Falling off didn't hurt me. I'm sorry about your cousin. It must have been so hard for you."

Dominic let go of her hand and put his arm around her shoulders. He didn't want her to move away. Her bare thigh was pressed up against his and what he wanted was only a breath away. He dipped his head, closed his eyes and lowered his mouth to hers.

Maybe it was a kiss returned because she felt sorry for him—maybe not. All he knew was that her lips were sweet beneath his and he explored her mouth gently. She sighed his name and her breath whispered against his lips. Jilly reached up and her fingers tangled in his wet hair as she pulled him closer. There was more than sympathy in her response. He groaned against her mouth and pushed her gently back on the sand.

By the time he had kissed her lips, her face, and then slowly slid his lips down her neck to that sweet spot he had noticed in the shadow of her collarbone, she was arching against him. Dominic lowered his hand to slip it inside her bikini top and cupped her in his palm as she murmured with pleasure against his neck. He lifted his head and looked down at her, her eyes were wide; she looked more alive than he had ever seen her. Passion filled her eyes and a slow smile tilted those lips that had been against his neck a few seconds ago. The sharp bark of a dog brought him to his senses, and he pulled back and straightened her top.

He rolled over and sat up and looped his hands around his knees. Luckily the dog had run ahead and the couple walking along the beach was still a couple of hundred metres away. Jilly sat up and brushed the sand from her shoulders.

He stared out to sea, breathing deeply as the couple walked along the beach towards them.

Not a word was spoken.

***

Jilly folded her arms across her chest. Her heart was beating at the rate of knots and she flicked a glance at Dominic. He was staring out to sea; his jaw hard. His gaze steely. So many sensations ran through her; it was more than the physical. Somehow, she knew that they had connected on a deeper level than sheer physical need. If it hadn't been for the dog barking, they would have been making love. She craved his touch and shivered as he shifted his position and put more distance between them.

The dog bounded up to them, a huge black thing with floppy ears and loose jowls. She laughed as it nuzzled into her neck, the same place that Dominic's lips had been only minutes before. She jumped to her feet as the dog played around them, and she knew the exact second that Dominic turned to look at her, even though she wasn't watching him. She felt his eyes on her like a brand. It was crazy but she did.

The couple whistled to their dog and waved to Dominic and Jilly as they walked away.

"Do you want to go back in the surf on my board or go back to the cottage?"

She tried to read what was in his voice and subdue the restlessness that was in her. It was hard to quell, that deep ache low in her belly and the tingling down low made it hard to think logically.

She tried to lighten the mood. "How about some plum pudding for breakfast? It is Boxing Day."

His smile was distant and the warm feeling in her shriveled. He'd started it and she'd made a fool of herself. Dominic stood and together they picked up their boards and headed back toward the cottages.

Her heart was still thudding in slow, heavy beats and the blood was zinging around her body. Her nerve endings were skittering all over the place as confusion filled her. But when they reached the road, Dominic turned to face her.

"Sorry the surfing was such a fiasco. We'll try again another morning, okay?" He hitched the board up higher and nodded at her. "Have a good day; I have to go to Coffs Harbour. Anything you need?"

Jilly shook her head. "No, thank you."

She watched him as he walked away, before she turned and went back to her place. This holiday was not working out how she'd planned. It was time to forget about Dominic and try to relax and have the rest she'd planned. It had been a long time since she'd made out on a beach, but the frustration that filled her had more to do with Dominic's hot and cold moods than any unfulfilled sexual needs.

The day passed slowly. No matter how much Jilly tried to push him from her mind, Dominic wouldn't leave her thoughts. She'd come here for the quiet and today, she got in—in bucket loads. She read and dozed and took herself off for a long walk down to

Valla Beach after lunch. Burned off the chocolate, the strawberry milk and the beer. The cottage up the road stayed quiet and empty and there was no sign of Dominic's silver car.

When she came back from her walk, she settled gingerly in the hammock chair with a cold drink and her Kindle. She looked around nervously as she plumped up the cushions. No wind this afternoon. She pushed her foot onto the floor and rocked the chair gently as she began to read.

"Who the hell are you?"

Jilly dropped her Kindle with a start and slid out of the hammock as a woman clumped up the wooden steps. She strode along the verandah towards her, arms swinging wildly by her sides. It was hard to pick her age; her skin was tanned a deep nut-brown and her face was set in a ferocious glare. Her hair was looped up in some sort of old-fashioned beehive bun, she wore a pair of men's boardshorts and a bikini top and her feet were bare and encrusted with dirt. One hand pointed at Jilly, in the other was a small garden spade which she was now waving around.

119

Before Jilly could reply, she was hit with another spray of angry words. "What the hell are you doing in my brother's house?"

Jilly straightened and took a step back as the garden spade came perilously close to her head. The woman's dark eyes were fixed intently on her.

"I'm Jilly Henderson and I'm renting this house for the Christmas break."

"Says who?" The woman stepped closer.

"Says me. And I believe you are trespassing." Jilly lifted her chin as anger replaced fear. "Unless you can be civil, perhaps you should leave."

"No. I've come to weed the garden." She took a step back and pointed to the overgrown garden bed along the front fence.

Jilly's eyes narrowed. "Was it you who mowed the lawn yesterday."

"Yes, and I suppose it was your car that was in the way." Even though her face was unfriendly the woman had lowered her voice. "I washed my feet before I moved it.

Well at least that let Dominic off the hook. He

120

had been telling her the truth all along.

"Was it you who left me the flowers? On the kitchen table?"

"No. I didn't leave them for you. They were for my brother."

"Your brother?"

"Yes, Derek. I guess he was the one who organized the rental. I'm sorry for intruding. I'll leave the garden till you move out. How long are you here?"

"Another three days."

"Okay. Sorry to bother you, Jilly. I'm Margaret." She gave a shrill laugh as she went back down the steps and opened the gate. "They call me mad Margie but don't believe a word they say."

Jilly watched as Margaret strode along the road until she disappeared around the corner. This was the strangest vacation she had ever taken.

Maybe Vanuatu would have been more peaceful.

Although there'd be no Dominic there.

##

She showered early and dressed with care, blow-drying her hair into loose curls, wondering if—hoping—Dominic might come over for another sunset chat. She peered into the oval, cracked mirror above the small vanity in the outside toilet. Her skin had a healthy glow and the dark circles beneath her eyes had faded. Despite the unexpected and interesting events over the past couple of days, she was finally managing to relax.

The evening was cool; not a breath of wind disturbed the air tonight. Jilly sat on the steps of the verandah and enjoyed the peaceful setting as the sun set over the she-oaks. A rain bird called mournfully from the bush and then all was quiet. Dominic's house was in darkness and she thought back to the interlude on the beach this morning. They'd both made a mistake, not giving any thought to the conversation when they'd both agreed that work flings were definitely a no-go zone. Hopefully, they'd both put it behind them and forget about the kiss at the beach when they were back in the office.

Gradually the dark crept in and Jilly stood

slowly, ignoring the regret that filled her. A soft southerly wind puffed in off the ocean and her sarong wound around her legs as the breeze lifted it.

She shook her head. Sheer pleasure had filled her when Dominic had put his lips on hers and she wasn't going to regret one second of it. For the first time in many months she felt alive and if he was happy to spend some time with her, she'd welcome him into her life. They were two grownups and surely they could handle some time together out of work. The way Dominic had kissed her—and touched her—this morning, she knew he was interested. If it hadn't been for that dog...

It *was* lonely here by herself and she would enjoy his company again. Opening the fridge, she carried some salad leaves inside and sat at the table listening for his car.

But nothing.

Finally, after a light meal she changed into her PJs and climbed into bed. She hadn't even heard his car come back when she fell asleep just before midnight. The only sound was the soft sighing of the waves through the trees as they washed up on the beach.

When Jilly woke with a start it was pitch dark. She lay there for a moment listening and wondering what had woken her. She shivered; there was a chill in the room. Goose bumps rose on her bare skin and the hair on the back of her neck lifted. Her mouth dried as the other side of the bed dipped and she rolled toward the centre of the bed.

She tensed as a hand crept onto her hip.

"Dominic?" Her throat was dry, and the words came out raspy and sleepy.

"Heh heh." The same soft chuckle she had heard on the verandah turned her blood to ice.

Pulling all her courage together, she swallowed and reached over. Taking a deep breath and trying to stay calm she placed her hand on the warm fingers that still rested lightly against her hip.

"Who are you?" She pulled the shaky words from that nervous place in her chest at the same time she pushed her fingernails into the hand now holding her firmly. The man chuckled again, and the bed dipped again as he rolled away. Jilly rolled over in one fluid movement and was on her feet, reaching for the light before she could even draw a breath. She clicked the switch, bathing the room in bright white light, and she looked around for something to use as a weapon.

There was no one in the room with her and the door was still shut. Drawing in a shaky breath, she walked around to the other side of the bed and bent down, looking underneath.

Nobody. Nothing. The only thing in the room was a chill that raised the goose bumps on her arms. Jilly grabbed a blanket off the bed and backed into the chair in the corner, her eyes fixed on the door in front of her.

***

Dominic came in late, his thoughts churning. Kissing Jilly at the beach had been a stupid thing to do; it had been her sympathy and wide eyes that had weakened him to her charms. God, if it hadn't been for that slobbery dog, he probably would have ripped her white bikini off and made love to her on the sand. His hard and fast rule of non-involvement at work would have been broken irrevocably because he knew once he had a taste of making love to Jilly, there was no way he'd be able to hold back. He had to work with her, and he was not going to get involved with someone at the office.

Mr. Iceberg he would stay. He knew the nickname the girls had given him, and it suited him just fine. But the feel of Jilly's breast beneath his hand and the taste of her salty skin on his lips had stayed with him all day. Not trusting himself to keep his hands off her, he'd gone for a long drive, telling himself he was simply checking out the surf up the coast.

A stupid move; he'd got caught in the Boxing Day traffic and had been held up on the highway until well after dark. The other cottage was in darkness and he guessed Jilly was asleep when he finally drove past, resisting the temptation to call in and check on her.

Three more days; he'd keep his distance and when they were back in Sydney, nothing would be changed and there'd be no messy holiday romance to get over.

That's what his head told him anyway; his heart was saying something different as the blood hammered though his body. Another cold shower was in order.

After he parked the car, he pushed open his own front door in disgust and threw the keys onto the table. He went to bed and tossed and turned until a restless sleep over took him.

Chapter Eleven
December 27

In the early dawn, the southerly wind strengthened, and the bathroom door clicked on and off its latch until Dominic couldn't put up with it any longer. He yawned and sat on the edge of the bed rubbing his eyes.

"Tired, mate?"

The familiar voice hit Dominic in the gut. He dropped his hands and slowly lifted his head. Derro was lounging back in the chair beside the bed, smiling at him, his tanned face crinkled around the eyes so like his own.

Hell. Dominic rubbed his eyes again.

His cousin, his *dead* cousin, sat in the chair dressed in his familiar faded denims and favourite Metallica T-shirt. They'd gone to that concert in Sydney for Dominic's eighteenth birthday. Derro took a bite from the apple he was holding. The sweet smell of the juice drifted over to Dominic along with the loud crunch.

"Don't stress. It's cool."

Crunch, as he bit the apple again.

"Derro?" Dominic's voice was a ragged whisper. "Shit, I'm dreaming, aren't I?"

"Nup, no dream. It's me, man."

The familiar grin tore at Dominic's chest and he took a deep breath. "Really?"

The cheeky nod he knew so well confirmed it.

"Yeah. I've been keeping an eye out for you and you're sure stuffing things up."

"What? Where?"

"Are you really happy being a suit, Dom?" Derro stood and walked around the table and pegged the apple core into the bin.

Do ghosts eat apples? Or am I dreaming?

Dominic stood and resisted pinching himself. He looked down at the bed. He wasn't lying there asleep. He was awake and talking to his dead cousin.

"Shit, Derro. Why did you have to go and drown? Do you know how much I missed you?"

129

"It was my time, Dom. But I had to come back and sort you out before I can move on. Couldn't let you stuff up too."

"What happened?"

Derro's face split into a wide grin. "Caught the best wave of my life, man. A six-foot left hander on the point. Perfect tube, but I didn't pull out in time."

Dominic shook his head, still unable to believe what he was seeing and hearing.

"So enough about me. I'm fine. I'm here to give you a bit of advice."

Dominic stared at his cousin. "Advice?" He cleared his throat and the words rasped out.

"Don't let her go. Don't let that stupid career, and figures and money drive your life. Jilly's the one for you, mate. I used Margie's email to set up the rental. That was interesting." He walked to the window and turned back to Dominic. "I've done my best to throw you together, but it's up to you now. You have to decide what *you* want."

Dominic knew what he wanted, and it had nothing to do with suits and the trading floor. Derro smiled at him as he read his expression; he knew him well and always had.

"Good." Derro turned back to Dominic. "Want to go for a surf later? I'll be out there with you if you go."

Dominic's throat ached and he blinked as a sheen of moisture misted his eyes. "I wish."

"Look out for Margie, mate. Tell her I'm okay. She's still doin' it tough too." Derro walked over and grabbed him in a tight man hug. "Have a good life, Dom."

Gradually the pressure of his arms lessened, and Dominic opened his eyes. The room was empty, and he looked around.

"What the hell?" he muttered as he flopped onto the bed and put his hands over his eyes. He leaned back onto the soft pillow and closed his eyes as the wind rattled around the house.

A persistent banging at the door woke him a couple of hours later. The dream had been so real; he still carried the same sense of loss in his chest that he'd experienced when Derro had left him.

131

Maudlin. That's what he was. Dreaming of the past. Time to go back to the city and his real life. Dominic rolled out of bed and had the door open before he was properly awake. Jilly stood there, her face pale and dark shadows beneath her eyes.

"Hi, come on in."

She stepped past him without speaking, and stood there looking at him, before she brushed a shaky hand over her face. She was dressed in a cute pair of pyjamas and he raised his eyebrows.

"You are going to think I am so crazy, but this really strange thing happened to me last night." Her voice was soft and her green eyes wide as she stared up at him

"You're not Robinson Crusoe." Calm settled over Dominic as he looked her. Derro—or his dream—whatever it had been, had given him a choice. He put his hands on her shoulders, surprised to feel her trembling. "So shush, and listen to me. I'm sorry I was such a grouch yesterday and took off and left, but you scare me."

"Scared? Tell me about it."

"What's wrong?" Her skin was silky against his fingertips as he ran them down her arms.

"I was frightened last night, too."

Dominic groaned and he narrowed his eyes. "Don't tell me you had a dream too?"

"No, I had a flesh and blood visitor. I thought it was you, until he chuckled. And then he disappeared." Jilly's eyes were wide. "I was so scared I spent the rest of the night sitting up in a chair. I don't know what it was but there was definitely someone in the house."

"Just give me a moment." Dominic crossed to the kitchen and lifted the top of the bin. He shook his head as disbelief ran through him; a fresh apple core lying at the bottom of the plastic-lined bin. Maybe he'd put it there without remembering?

He turned back to Jilly and took her arm gently before leading her over to the bed. "You do look tired. Do you want to go back to bed? Get some sleep?" He grinned at her as her eyes locked with his. Enough of the stuffed shirt businessman. Dominic, the wild surfer without any worries, had come roaring back.

Thank you, coz.

From now on, the risks he took would have nothing to do with trades and shares. He sat on the edge of the bed and held his arms out and could have sworn he heard a chuckle as Jilly sat on his knee.

"Shut the door on the way out, Derro," he said quietly.

##

Certain that Dominic would hear the thudding of her heart Jilly leaned into him as his arms went around her waist.

"Back to bed? Here?" Her voice was tentative. "You're not going to go all cold on me again?"

A warm feeling suffused her as a rumble of laughter vibrated against her chest. "No, trust me. I had a very good lesson through the night." She frowned as he glanced over to the bin. "Mr. Iceberg's gone for good this time."

This time the heat was from embarrassment and she pulled back and stared at him. "How did you know that's what they call you at work?"

134

Dominic laughed again. "I wondered if you knew that the walls between my office and the staff room are very thin." He bent his knee and waggled his foot in the air in front of them. "That Shaz has some interesting theories."

Jilly stared at him, the heat in her face warring for supremacy with the heat that was building in her girlie parts. "You hear everything?"

"Everything." His lips zoomed in on her warm neck and her breath caught in her throat.

Choking out a strangled laugh, she shivered as his fingers slid down and held the bottom of her pajama top. "Oh my God, how embarrassing!"

"But you, Miss Henderson, are always most circumspect in your conversations with your work friends." He tipped his head to the side with raised eyebrows and Jilly nodded. She closed her eyes as the soft cotton brushed her face when he lifted the top over her head.

"Are you sure?" He leaned forward and nuzzled his lips into her neck

Confidence surged through Jilly and she gave

him a wicked smile. "I guess I won't be sure Mr. Iceberg has really gone unless you share some body heat with me."

Jilly couldn't help the small giggle that escaped as she looked down at his feet. He lifted his head. "What?"

"Nothing." She shook her head. "Just testing out a theory or two."

"And?"

Again, a little giggle. "You do have big . . . feet."

"I aim to please." Dominic lifted her off his lap and laid her on the bed. Jilly lay there admiring the play of the muscles in his thighs as he bent down. She closed her eyes.

God, was this a dream too? If it was, she was going to enjoy every moment of it. A snap of foil and he was back beside her, the warmth of his skin against her body heating her from shoulder to toe.

Unfamiliar emotion flooded her. "Definitely not Mr. Iceberg," she murmured.

***

Dominic knew he'd remember the little sounds

coming from Jilly's lips for the rest of his life. He cupped her hips, loving the feel of her soft curves against him.

"Warm enough now?" he murmured against her neck. He kissed her shoulder and traced his lips to the nape of her neck.

"Not an iceberg to be seen," she said with a sexy giggle.

He fell asleep with Jilly's legs wrapped around his, holding him close.

Chapter Twelve
New Year's Eve

Jilly rolled over and propped her head on her elbow. Dominic was sleeping peacefully beside her, his broad chest rising gently with his breathing. She had moved her few things into his cottage when he'd locked up his cousin's cottage three days ago. She reached out and tucked a stray curl behind his ear, but he didn't stir. The last few days had been wonderful. She'd done more wild things with him this week than she had in her whole life. Beach sex. Up against the wall sex. Morning Sex. Afternoon sex and one all night marathon session. Luckily Dominic had filled his fridge with groceries because her appetite was insatiable. Not only for him, but for food as well.

Eating, sleeping, surfing, and sex. A magic vacation. She grinned to herself—maybe magic wasn't the right word to use. He'd driven into town and brought his cousin Margaret back for lunch on their second last day. Margie was quirky but friendly to Jilly, especially

138

once she knew that Derro's cottage was empty again. She'd bolted down her lunch and borrowed a garden spade from Dominic's shed, preferring to weed the garden than catch up on old times with her cousin and his—

His what? Jilly wondered.

His executive assistant? His girlfriend? His lover? A quiver of uncertainty ran through her as she wondered what things would be like when they returned to Sydney.

All doubts fled when Dominic opened his eyes and reached for her. His lips found hers before she could speak but Dominic said all there was to say without words.

##

"How do you want to greet the New Year?" Dominic came up behind her in the kitchen as she washed some lettuce leaves in the old sink. "Mary at the servo tells me there's a rocking party at the river."

"What river?"

His deep laugh sent a shiver though her. She'd fallen hard for this man over the past few days.

Working with him for the last six months, although distant, had already shown her what a good man he was. He was a man of integrity, kind and considerate. This week had also shown her what a great sense of humor he possessed . . . and what a versatile lover he was.

"The one around the point."

"Didn't know there was one. You've barely let me out of bed."

"Are you complaining, Miss Henderson? Am I working you too hard again?"

"I'm not. But tonight's our last night before we go back to the big smoke and I think I'd rather stay in unless you want to go out?" She turned around and held his gaze steadily. "What's going to happen when we go back to work? What about our rules?"

"I've had an idea and our rules aren't going to matter." Jilly looked up at him, but he wouldn't be drawn into discussing his idea.

He shook his head. "Come on, we'll head into the shops and get some food and I'll cook you a fabulous meal. Tempt you with some local seafood,

140

perhaps?"

"Tempt me? I don't need seafood for that. Maybe some whipped cream and strawberries? What do you think of that?" she said in a husky voice.

"Mm. Maybe ice cream? Your skin is feeling very hot."

They made the local shops five minutes before closing time.

***

New Year's Day

Rested and relaxed, Dominic and Jilly packed his Audi ready for the trip back to Sydney together later that afternoon. For some reason, her car was stone dead and she knew Dominic suspected that a well-meaning—but ghostly—hand had been at work. He had insisted that they needed to have a midday nap to prepare for the trip ahead, but of course very little sleep had taken place. She shook her head and her hair brushed against his shoulder, but his eyes remained closed as his chest rose and fell gently.

If anyone had told her the events that would pass

when she came for her solitary holiday at the beach, she would have told them they had had a touch of sun, or perhaps too much Christmas cheer. But Dominic's explanation had been heartfelt and had supported the things that had happened to her over the past few days; Jilly wondered whether a ghostly influence really had been at work bringing them together. Or was it simply that their deepest desires had culminated in dreams that had guided their choices.

She would never forget that night of terror sitting up in the chair when something had frightened her out of the cottage and into Dominic's arms. She moved to lie back on her pillow, but her hand was held and pressed against a tanned and golden-haired chest. She sighed and smiled into the wicked eyes that were holding hers and she gave into the exquisite sensation that ran through her whenever he touched her. Anywhere, anytime—even a touch on her back as he walked behind her sent shimmers of desire running straight through her. She let out a little giggle.

"What's so funny?" Dominic's fingers were

doing wicked things to Jilly's composure as they moved down her back. She rolled over and lay on top of him.

She smiled at him and kept her tone saucy. "I was just thinking about the size of your feet and whether I should tell Shaz about her theory."

"Don't you dare." His voice was husky as he moved his lips down the side of her neck.

"I'll be able to tell the girls that I have tested the theory and that Mr. Iceberg has a new nickname. Mr. Hot Stuff, maybe?" She giggled at the look on his face as he pulled her down to his chest.

"Oh, I don't think so, Miss Henderson. I think you'll be doing exactly what your boss says."

And Jilly did for the next hour or two.

"I've got a proposition for you," Dominic said later that afternoon.

Jilly threw him a laughing glance. "We don't have time."

"I'm serious." He walked across to her.

She tilted her head to the side. His face was

143

closed, and he looked more like Dominic the boss. Zipping up her toiletries bag, she put it on the bed and walked across to him. She slipped her arms around his waist, reveling in her new-found ease with this man.

"Tell me."

"How much do you like living in Sydney?"

"I don't. I'd be out of there like a shot if I could get a decent job out of the city."

"How would you like to be my executive assistant in another business? Out of the city?"

Hope flowed through her as she stared up at him.

"Where?"

"How about here? We can do what we do from anywhere, you know. There's more to life than work and with our experience, we could work from here and use our skills consulting and telecommuting in the finance industry."

"And surf some of the day?"

A slow grin crossed his face as she looked up at him and saw her expression.

"Amongst other physical activities."

In the end they decided to leave Jilly's car there; it was a good excuse to come up for another weekend and start to set up their home office until they were replaced at the bank. Dominic's Audi was packed with their bags, and both surfboards were secured to the roof racks.

"We'll have to surf at Narrabeen until we move back," he said. "You can't let all that surfing practice go to waste." He locked the front door of the cottage and walked slowly along the verandah. Jilly waited for him in the car and he smiled as she caught his eye.

"Hurry up. It's hot in the car." She waved a hand in front of her face in an exaggerated movement. "Come on and get those big feet walking over here, boss."

Dominic smiled back at her. "Whatever you say, Miss Henderson."

Dominic had no doubt that in some way, Derro—whether it had been a dream or not—had shown him the way to where his future and true happiness lay.

With Jilly. At the beach.

He slipped into the driver's seat and started the car. Slowly he drove down the driveway and glanced in the rear-view mirror, back at the cottage where he had spent many happy years, and where he was going to make a life with Jilly. He touched her hand and gestured back behind them.

Though the haze of the late afternoon, Derro leaned against the fence, his surfboard beneath his arm. Lazily, he lifted his arm and waved before he turned and walked across the sandy road to the beach, disappearing into the sea mist that hadn't been there a moment before.

THE END

I hope you've enjoyed *Christmas With the Boss*

Turn the page for other books and series by
Annie Seaton

Whitsunday Dawn

CHRISTMAS WITH THE BOSS

Undara

Porter Sisters Series

Kakadu Sunset
Daintree
Diamond Sky
Hidden Valley Sunrise (2020)

Pentecost Island Series (2020)

Pippa

Eliza

Nell

Tamsin (June)

Evie (July)

Bondi Beach Love Series
Beach House

Beach Music

Beach Walk

Beach Dreams

Prickle Creek Series

Her Outback Cowboy

Her Outback Surprise

His Outback Nanny

His Outback Temptation

Second Chance Bay Series

Her Outback Playboy

Her Outback Protector

Her Outback Haven

Her Outback Paradise

Love Across Time Series

Come Back to Me

Follow Me

Lucy's Story (2020)

Others

The Trouble with Paradise

The Trouble with Jack (April)

Deadly Secrets

Adventures in Time

Silver Valley Witch

The Emerald Necklace

Ten Days in Tuscany

Worth the Wait

Full Circle

About the Author

Author of the Year Ausrom Readers' Choice 2014

Best Established Author Ausrom Readers' Choice 2015

Finalist for Author of the Year, Book of the Year, Cover of the Year, Ausrom Readers' Choice 2016

Best Established Author, Ausrom Readers' Choice 2017

Book of the Year. Ausrom Readers' Choice 2018

Annie lives in Australia, on the beautiful north coast of New South Wales. She sits in her writing chair and looks out over the tranquil Pacific Ocean. She has fulfilled her lifelong dream of becoming an author and is producing books at a prolific rate.

She writes contemporary romance and loves telling the stories that always have a happily ever after. She lives with her very own hero of many years and they share their home with Toby, the naughtiest dog in the universe, and Barney, the rag doll kitten, who hides when the grandchildren come to visit.

Stay up to date with her latest releases at her website: http://www.annieseaton.net

If you would like to stay up to date with Annie's releases, subscribe to her newsletter on her website